"Get out!" yelled Smirk as the time machine seemed about to explode. Likewise, inside the *Endocrine,* Dacron herded the other crewmembers out the exit, where they slid down the inflated emergency slide.

Everyone gathered nearby and turned back to stare at the travel crafts, which were vibrating faster and faster, until they disappeared.

The crewmembers became aware that they were not alone; a tremendous crowd of people surrounded them. Recovering from their shock, the crew looked around at where they'd landed.

It was a huge convention hall in a modern hotel. A banner off to the side read, "Welcome, Wrekkies."

The thought struck all of them, even Piker, at the same instant: they had been thrown into the future, right into the middle of the wrekkie convention they'd seen on the Preview. . . .

STAR WRECK III
Time Warped
A PARODY

St. Martin's Paperbacks Titles by Leah Rewolinski

STAR WRECK: THE GENERATION GAP

STAR WRECK II: THE ATTACK OF THE JARGONITES

STAR WRECK III: TIME WARPED

STAR WRECK II
TIME WARPED

A Parody—Then, Now and Forever

by

LEAH REWOLINSKI

ILLUSTRATIONS BY HARRY TRUMBORE

A 2M COMMUNICATIONS LTD. PRODUCTION

SMP
ST. MARTIN'S PAPERBACKS

Star Wreck is an unauthorized parody of the *Star Trek* television and motion picture series, and the *Star Trek: The Next Generation* television series. None of the individuals or companies associated with these series or with any merchandise based upon these series, has in any way sponsored, approved, endorsed or authorized this book.

Published by arrangement with the author

STAR WRECK III: TIME WARPED

Cover illustration by Bob Larkin.

ISBN: 0-312-92891-2

Printed in the United States of America

St. Martin's Paperbacks edition/October 1992

10 9 8 7 6 5 4 3 2 1

To Tom, my fellow time traveler

Acknowledgments

Thanks to two people who helped make this book possible: associate publisher Janine Coughlin of St. Martin's Press, with her genuine enthusiasm and support; and my agent, Madeleine Morel, whose classy British accent inspires me to new literary heights.

For research assistance, thanks to Jack Ratajczyk for lending me his tape of "The City on the Edge of Forever."

Thanks to Gimli for staying by my side during the writing of this manuscript.

And thanks to Brent Spiner, one of the most talented actors I've never met, for inspiration.

Contents

1 Here We Go Again 1
2 A Ship Divided 19
3 Déjà Boo-Boo 33
4 Bored Silly 41
5 Neuts to the Rescue 49
6 The Days and Nights of Yasha Tar 63
7 The City on the Edge of Foreclosure 70
8 Rescue Redux 80
9 Childhood's Dead End 87
10 That Was Then . . . This Is Nuts 94
11 On with the Show 103

1

Here We Go Again

"IT WAS THE best of times; it was the worst of times." Capt. James T. Smirk paused to read the line he'd just written. Then he crossed it out and wrote: "The times were OK." There. That was much better.

Only 598 more pages and I'll be done with these memoirs, Smirk thought. He closed his eyes and pictured his book occupying the "#1 bestseller" slot on the bookstore display. He could even envision his picture on the cover, just beneath the title: *So Many Classy Dames, So Little Time.*

Inspired, Smirk flourished his feather pen and straightened the parchment. Then he paused; what should he say next?

He knew that the autobiography would recount his dashing conquests of exotic alien races, fearsome creatures, and gorgeous women. Yet something was nagging at him.

Suddenly he realized what it was. Their current situation would make a boring chapter.

The crews of Capt. Smirk and Capt. Jean-Lucy Ricardo were back together again on the USS *Endocrine*. After the crews defeated the Jargonites—destroying Smirk's ship in the process—Starfreak Command ordered them to share Ricardo's ship and cooperate on future missions.

But the brass back at headquarters have no idea what

it's like out here in the field, Smirk thought. *Sharing this ship is the pits.* The members of Smirk's and Ricardo's crews bickered constantly, despite the captains' efforts to maintain peace. The infighting distracted everybody from their ongoing mission of finding novel predicaments to get into.

It was so much better when we didn't have to share a ship, Smirk thought. *If only we could go back in time and get my ship before it was blown up in the Jargonite war. Hey, wait a minute. We CAN go back in time. Yeah! And my crew could bring our ship to the present, and we'd be free again.*

There was just one hitch. Since Smirk's crew would need to build a time machine, Capt. Ricardo was bound to notice what they were up to. And Ricardo was notoriously reluctant to mess around with the space/time continuum.

He's so overprotective of history, Smirk thought. *So what if we change a few minor events? It always worked out all right before.*

Heck, it's worth a try. It shouldn't be that hard to persuade Ricardo to let us go. I'm sure he'd do anything to get us out of his hair, such as it is.

Smirk decided to propose the project immediately. However, he knew better than to call a formal meeting to discuss it. He'd never seen a starship where meetings got so out of hand as on the *Endocrine.* Capt. Ricardo was apt to invite everyone who wanted to get their two cents in, even people like Dr. Flusher who had absolutely nothing to contribute.

Instead, Smirk decided, he wouldn't even use the term "meeting." He'd just invite Ricardo to a friendly discussion. And he realized his right-hand man Mr. Smock should be there, too, just in case he needed some actual thought to bolster his argument.

Smirk reached for the intercom microphone, then remembered that they didn't have one. All he had to do was page Capt. Ricardo, and the computer would find him.

At that moment Ricardo was in the ship's lounge, Ten-Foreplay, mulling over a command decision: what to order for lunch.

Should he have Earl Grape tea and buttered crumpets, as he'd eaten for lunch every day since the Battle of Hastings? Or should he vary his routine and spread marmalade on the crumpets instead? A wave of anxiety washed over him, with vague yet terrifying fears over the consequences of switching to marmalade.

Then he shook his head and thought, *Perhaps Counselor Troit is right. I* AM *becoming rather compulsive.*

"You subconsciously resent having to share command of your ship," Troit had advised him, "so you seek a sense of control over your life by performing these compulsive behaviors."

At the time, Capt. Ricardo had ignored her diagnosis. He regretted telling her that every night after his bedtime shower and skull-polishing, he went around the ship checking that all 1,476 stove burners were shut off, 589 toasters were unplugged and 1,225 sets of drapes were closed. "You can't be too careful," Ricardo had told Troit.

Troit had also observed that his command style was beginning to fossilize. She'd pointed out, "Do you realize that yesterday you said 'Make it so' 53 times?" She'd given him some worry beads to play with, which helped for a while.

But now, Ricardo thought, *compulsion is rearing its ugly head once again. No, wait, that's just my reflection in the mirror behind the bar. Well, I'll show her. I'll do something wild and radical to break with the past.*

The waitress arrived at his table and began a singsong recital of the day's special: "Today's featured item is broiled fillet of sole with potatoes au gratin and fresh broccoli . . . but—no, don't tell me, let me guess—you're going to have Earl Grape tea and buttered crumpets."

Capt. Ricardo flashed what he hoped was a devil-may-care grin and responded, "No. I've decided to live dangerously. Make it sole."

While waiting for his order, Capt. Ricardo ventured even further on the wild side by sampling the cellophane-wrapped sesame crackers in the breadbasket. As usual, he started counting so he could chew the mouthful exactly 23 times before swallowing, but then the intercom distracted him.

"Jean-Lucy." It was Capt. Smirk's voice. "I'd like to discuss something with you. Let's get together in your Ready Room at 2560 hours, okay?"

Ricardo started to object—this get-together sounded like it had formal meeting potential—but the cracker crumbs caught in his throat. He coughed and wheezed. Smirk took this for a "Yes" and signed off the intercom.

Ricardo continued to hack as the dusty cracker crumbs lodged in his windpipe. His face turned scarlet; diners at nearby tables looked on with increasing concern. One of them jumped up and encircled Ricardo's chest to perform the Heimlich maneuver. He squeezed with terrific force—expelling the cracker, and Ricardo's false teeth as well.

Mr. Smock was bored. How bored was he? He was so bored that, just to have something to do, he was about to read a book he'd sworn he would never read . . . the book he'd been avoiding since the day he first saw it in the *Endocrine*'s library . . . the book that now remained as the single volume in the entire library that he hadn't read:

14,000 Things to Be Sappy About.

He tried to psych himself up before opening the cover. Surely it couldn't be as bad as it sounded. Maybe a little bit of whimsy was just what he needed. Summoning up more courage, he flipped through the pages at random. Out of the corner of his eye he peeked at a few entries:

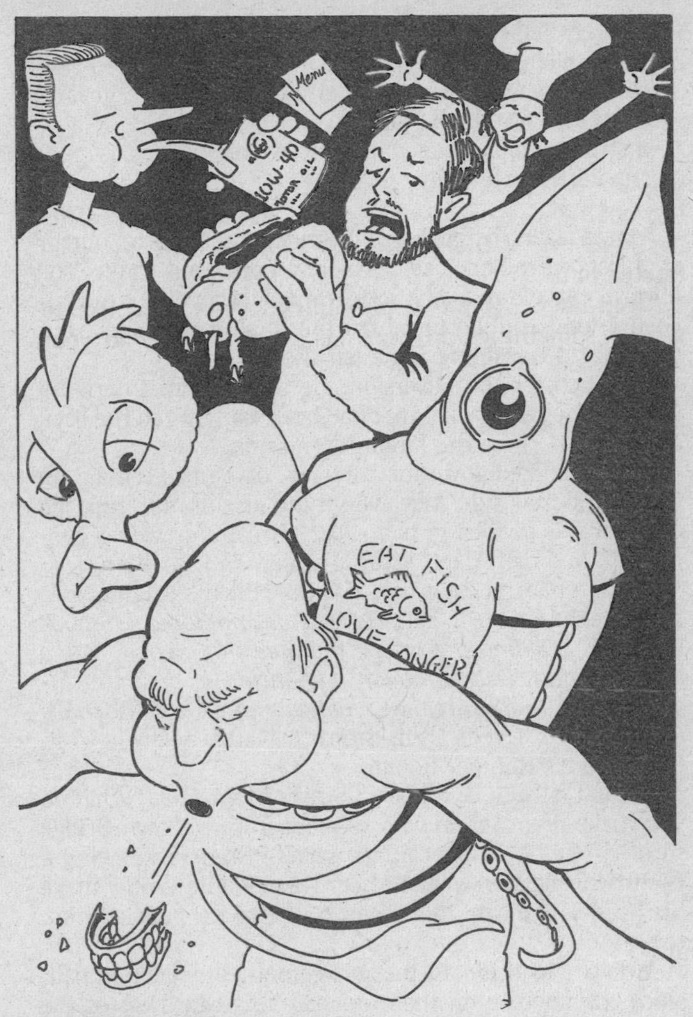

One of them jumped up and encircled Ricardo's chest to perform the Heimlich maneuver.

rubbery Jell-O salads with canned fruit in them
torn undergarments
the giddy, wispy way you feel when the alarm goes off at 5 A.M. on a Monday
a strong enema on a wintry afternoon
the Partridge Family

"Aaaaaaaaarrrrrgggghhhh!" Smock recoiled in horror and dropped the book as if it were a poisonous snake. The librarian gave him a dirty look. Smock recovered his composure long enough to return the book to the shelf, but he was still trembling as he left the library.

So much for that diversion. He didn't want to end up wearing the straitjacket that had been hanging in the back of his closet since the Jargonite mission.

Smock walked down the corridor, careful to remain on the Smirk-crew side. Like everything else on the ship, the corridor was divided in half. Capt. Smirk's crew was confined to one half, Capt. Ricardo's crew to the other.

It was a natural extension of Cmdr. Piker's original idea to divide the Bridge in half. *Yet that was not logical,* Smock reflected. *Dividing the Bridge put steering control in the hands of our crew, although navigation is on Capt. Ricardo's side. And so are the Crewmover and Capt. Ricardo's Ready Room.* Or, as Capt. Smirk privately referred to it, the captain's Romper Room.

"I can't fathom it, Smock," Smirk often said. "What do you make of a captain who retreats from his own Bridge so often? Is he anti-social, or what?" Smock, knowing a rhetorical question when he heard one, would simply shake his head to indicate that Ricardo's behavior puzzled him, too.

Awkward as this was, the ship remained divided in half, since the majority of the crew had voted in favor of the idea. It wasn't too bad in the laundromat, the mall, or even Ten-Foreplay, but things got a little strange in the showers, where the "cold" faucets were on Smirk's side

Like everything else on the ship, the corridor was divided in half.

and the "hot" on Ricardo's. Ricardo's crew frequently suffered third-degree burns, while Smirk's crew tended toward pneumonia.

As for Cmdr. Piker, who originated this brilliant scheme, Smock had a plan. For the past few months Smock had been secretly sending Piker's resume to dozens of starships throughout the galaxy, hoping that someone would hire him away from the *Endocrine.* The ploy had resulted in a surprising number of offers. But so far, to Smock's disappointment, Piker had turned them all down.

The intercom broke into Smock's train of thought. "Smirk here, Mr. Smock. Capt. Ricardo and I are getting together at 2560 hours in the Romper—er, Ready Room to discuss an idea of mine. Why don't you join us?"

"Certainly, Captain," Smock responded. *Anything to break the monotony,* he thought.

"Oh, and Smock," Smirk continued, "don't mention to Ricardo the reason we're meeting, all right?"

"I will not, Captain," said Smock, "especially since you have not told me what it is."

"Never mind," Smirk said. "I'll brief you on it before we go in. Just back me up, no matter what I say. Throw in a few facts and figures whenever there's a lull. Make it sound, you know, scientific."

Cmdr. Wilson Piker sat in his quarters, idly tugging at his beard, and finally admitted to himself that he was stumped.

Just as I expected, he thought. *The situation is much worse than I expected.*

For the past several hours he'd searched for a missing videotape. It was time to give up and admit that the darned thing was probably lost forever.

The video was a gift from Ensign Westerly Flusher, who had filmed a typical *Endocrine* workday as his 29th audition tape for Starfreak Academy Film School. To the crew's immense relief, the school finally accepted him. Westerly was now away at the Academy, majoring in cinematography and minoring in weeniehood.

Hmmmm. If I were a videotape, where would I be? Piker wondered. *Probably not serving as First Officer of a starship.*

Piker's train of thought jumped the track. *Even being First Officer isn't going to help me this time,* he fretted. *Usually, all I have to do is yell at somebody, and the problem gets solved.*

Why, just the day before they'd had some serious trouble with the water softener. Georgie LaForgery, trying to explain why the whirlpool baths were filling with crud, said Engineering would need at least four hours for repairs. "We haven't got four hours!" Piker had barked; and Georgie had fixed the softener in 45 minutes.

There was something magical about the way Piker asserted his authority. An impossible job became possible, solely because he demanded it. He was the only one on the ship with this talent, which was probably why Capt. Ricardo hadn't canned him long ago.

But I can't yell at somebody this time, because I'm the one who lost the video, Piker ruminated. *Let's see... where did I have it last?*

He remembered that he was about to watch the tape earlier that day. He'd just turned on the VCR when Capt. Ricardo had called on the intercom, reminding him to reset the ship's clocks for Daylight Saving Time.

I took the videotape with me to the computer room, Piker thought, *and put it on the counter next to my keychain. Then I reset all the clocks simultaneously with that new software, SpringAhead/FallBack. When I woke up on the floor, I picked up my keychain and left the computer room.*

Piker went over the scenario in his mind several times. Something about it bothered him. After several more minutes of intensely arduous thought, he figured out what it was: *Why did I wake up on the floor?*

"Computer," Piker said, "when I used the SpringAhead/

FallBack software this morning, were there any unusual effects?"

"Affirmative," said the computer's feminine voice.

"What happened?"

"The software contained a bug which created a time rift lasting 1.53 seconds."

Uh-oh, Piker thought. "Describe the effects of the time rift," he ordered.

"Momentary unconsciousness for sixteen officers; three unexplained pregnancies; the passage of a T-120 VHS videocassette into the abyss; and a loss of $1,435 in accrued interest on the ship's credit union accounts."

Geez. "About that videocassette—exactly where is it now?"

"Working," said the computer as it searched its records. After a pause, the computer announced, "Gone."

Beep-beep boop-boop, the door chime sounded in Capt. Ricardo's Ready Room. He made a mental note to have the melody reprogrammed to something more dignified—"Hail to the Chief," perhaps.

"Come," Ricardo answered.

Capt. Smirk and Mr. Smock entered. Ricardo felt a twinge of surprise; Smirk hadn't said anything about having Smock join in this discussion. It was probably some kind of ploy to catch him off-guard, Ricardo decided, so he'd retaliate by pretending not to mind.

"Ah, gentlemen," said Ricardo, leading them toward the lounge chairs arranged around a kidney-shaped coffee table. "Make yourselves comfortable, won't you?" Ricardo settled into a chair, wincing a little as he inadvertently leaned against the arm of the chair with his Heimlich-bruised ribs.

After the other two sat down, Ricardo picked up the candy dish and held it out to them. "Marzipan?"

"Thank you." Capt. Smirk smiled and took a piece of

the candy, which was molded in the shape of a Kringle torture rod.

"Mr. Smock?" offered Ricardo, tilting the dish toward him.

"No, thank you, Captain," responded Smock, folding his hands in his lap. "I do not eat sweets."

"Well, Capt. Smirk, what was it you wanted to see me about?" Capt. Ricardo said, attempting a smile which he hoped looked genuine; he'd been practicing all evening.

Smirk's first impulse was to propose his time travel idea right off the bat; but on the way over to the Ready Room Mr. Smock had advised him to open the discussion on neutral territory. So Smirk pretended this was just another problem-solving session on the captains' toughest problem: the bickering between their crews.

"Have you seen the warning letter from Starfreak's HMO?" Smirk asked. Ricardo nodded grimly. The letter stated that the *Endocrine* crew was way over the allowable number of claims for scalpel puncture wounds and I.V.-stand concussions. The injuries were occurring to patients who'd come to Sickbay for treatment and then got caught in the crossfire between Dr. McCaw and Dr. Beverage Flusher.

"What can we do about it?" Ricardo asked.

Smirk shrugged. "I can't tell Moans what to do. You know how bad his temper is. Any day now I expect to walk in there, find him kneeling over Flusher's body, and hear him say, 'She's dead, Jim.' "

Ricardo shuddered at the thought of Beverage being murdered. It was bad enough that he'd sent her husband Jock on that fatal Away Team mission years ago; now if Beverage also died under his command, it would look bloody awkward on his resume.

Smirk went on, "And did you know Wart broke Checkout's nose?"

"What?" Capt. Ricardo said. "When did that happen?"

"This afternoon. On the Bridge."

Injuries were occurring to patients who got caught between Dr. McCaw and Dr. Flusher.

"No, I didn't know," said Ricardo. "I've been here in my Ready Room since lunchtime." Smirk gave Smock a look that shouted, *See? What did I tell you?*

Smirk told Ricardo, "Smock saw how it all started. Could you repeat your report, Smock?"

"Certainly, Captain," said Mr. Smock. "In apparent retaliation for Lt. Wart's bullying, Mr. Zulu and Mr. Checkout had been throwing small magnets at his woven metal sash. They were keeping score of who got the most magnets to stick. Mr. Zulu was ahead five to three when the Kringle officer realized what was happening and charged them both."

"Uhhhhh," Ricardo moaned. Then he thought of another management problem. "I just got Security's damage report on that food fight in Ten-Foreplay last night," he said. "It seems your communications officer Yoohoo performed her lounge act one time too many. Let's see, I have the report here somewhere." Ricardo went to his desk, rummaged through piles of paper until he found the report, and brought it back to their chairs.

"Yes, here it is," he said, scanning the report. "Under 'Cause,' it reads, 'Chief bartender Guano, worried that Yoohoo's screeching was scaring away customers, threw out the first tomato as Yoohoo reached the chorus of 'To Dream the Impossible Dream.' "

"That was some fight," Smirk observed. "My shoulder is really sore. Smock, next time remind me to throw something smaller than a watermelon. So, Jean-Lucy, what does Security say about the total damage?"

"The upholstery on six chairs was stained," Ricardo read. "Also, a window was broken and three crewmembers were sucked out, along with some extremely valuable china."

"Mmmm. Tough break." They pondered the loss for a moment. Then Smirk said, "By the way, we're having another power outage tonight."

"Not again." Ricardo groaned. "Who's doing the sabotage this time, LaForgery or Snot?"

Yoohoo performed her lounge act one time too many.

"It's Mr. Snot," Smirk admitted. "But you can't blame him. You know he likes to keep that engineering stuff a secret; nobody else is supposed to know how it all works. Well, LaForgery wants to film a 'Reeking Rainbow' TV segment explaining the dilithium Crystal Vanish chamber."

Beep-beep boop-boop, the door chime sounded. "Come," said Ricardo, and Piker entered.

"Oops," said Piker. "I didn't realize you had company, Captain."

"That's all right, Number One." Ricardo motioned for him to sit down. "You can join us; the more the merrier. Pretty soon we'll have enough for a quorum. Does Dacron have the Bridge right now?"

"No," Piker answered. "Actually, I don't think anybody has the Bridge right now. Dacron's been missing since lunchtime."

"Missing. Again." Ricardo glared at Smock.

Smock stared back at him. "Why are you looking at *me,* Captain?" he deadpanned.

"Mr. Smock," Ricardo intoned, with an air of exaggerated patience, "I realize Mr. Dacron's constant babbling gets on your nerves. We've all felt similarly irritated with Dacron at one time or another. But most of us have refrained from flicking his 'off' switch and stashing him in a broom closet or a crawl space."

"What leads you to think I—" Smock protested.

"Why don't we all agree," Ricardo cut him off, "that if Dacron turns up at his station in one piece by morning, we'll let the matter drop with no questions asked. Shall we?"

"Very well, sir," Smock conceded.

Ricardo turned to Piker. "What brings you here, Number One?"

"Uh, just a minor problem with some software I was using, Captain. I'll tell you about it later when we're alone.

No sense boring Capt. Smirk and Mr. Smock with the details."

"Good idea," said Smirk. "Well, Jean-Lucy, as we were saying, it's fairly obvious that our crews aren't getting along."

"Hear, hear," murmured Ricardo.

"Things went much smoother when I had my old ship and we conducted our missions separately," Smirk continued.

"They certainly did," Ricardo assented.

"So, then, it's agreed," said Smirk, holding up his palms in his smoothest diplomatic gesture. Rapidly he concluded, "We'll go back in time, retrieve my ship before it was destroyed, and bring it to the present. Come on, Smock, let's get started." Smirk stood up and headed for the door.

"What?" Ricardo cried. "We will do no such thing!"

Smirk already had his back turned. Silently he mouthed, *Darn it all, darn it all, darnitalldarnitallDARNITALL.* He turned back to them. "Awww, c'mon, Jean-Lucy. For once in your life, don't be a wet blanket."

"Capt. Smirk," responded Ricardo, "interfering with the space/time continuum is inherently dangerous."

"That's just folklore," Smirk countered. "Actual scientific fact shows just the opposite. Isn't that right, Smock?"

"Er, yes, Captain," Smock chimed in. "Time travel has been proven safe and effective in 99 percent of all cases when combined with a closely-monitored program of oral hygiene and professional dental care."

"But you can never be sure," Ricardo insisted. "What if you accidentally introduce some new technology to the past? Or what if you interfere with a historically significant event? You could irreversibly alter the timeline which follows. The present as we know it might cease to exist."

"So what's so bad about that?" Smirk retorted. "The present as we know it could use some improvement, if you ask me. Heck, every time my crew went into the past, things turned out for the better."

"Oh, really?" Ricardo raised a skeptical eyebrow.

"Yes, really." Smirk waggled his head, imitating Ricardo's snooty look. "For instance, once we traveled back into a 1930s Earth timeline involving a woman named Edith Keebler, who had two possible fates. We made sure she got killed, just as she was supposed to. By doing that, we prevented the alternate timeline in which she would have become a famous peacenik—and so, thanks to us, the eventual result was World War II."

Ricardo gaped at Smirk. "You're saying you're responsible for World War II? You call that a good result?"

"Er, let me put that another way . . ." Smirk faltered. His face turned red as he muttered, "Smock, help me out here."

Unexpectedly, Piker broke in. "Sure, where would we be without World War II? If it hadn't happened, all of our present history books would be wrong." The other three, stunned by Piker's logic, stared at him.

Piker continued, "And if World War II never happened, there'd be no 'World at War' documentary to give Laurence Olivier his start as a narrator. Without that break, Olivier would probably be just another English actor doing voice-overs for Pontiac commercials."

Smirk felt a sinking sensation listening to Piker take his side, along with a twinge of sympathy for Ricardo, who worked with Piker on a daily basis.

Ricardo, meanwhile, glared his First Officer into silence. Icily he said, "Cmdr. Piker, could I see you in the conference room for a moment? Gentlemen, if you'll excuse us."

Ricardo and Piker left the Ready Room, crossed the Bridge, and entered the conference room. As soon as the doors slid shut, Ricardo hollered at Piker, "What do you think you're doing? Don't ever take sides with anyone against the Family again!"

Piker was surprised. Counselor Troit had told him the Captain was getting compulsive, but she hadn't said anything about paranoia.

"Now we haven't got a united front on this issue," Ricardo continued. "They'll keep badgering us until we let them have their way. If only we could prevent them from going back in time. Well, that's something I'll have to figure out. You, meanwhile, just keep a lid on it."

"Yes, sir." Piker kept his voice neutral, but inside he was seething. *Well, I may not be appreciated around here, but there are others who feel differently,* he thought. *Next time a headhunter calls, I might just listen.*

They returned to the Ready Room. Ricardo proposed, "Let's do this, Capt. Smirk: we'll use the Preview feature on the computer to find your ship in the past. At the same time, we'll have the computer analyze the possible effects on the space/time continuum of removing your ship from the past and bringing it to the present."

"Sounds good to me," Smirk agreed. "Let's start the mission, shall we?"

The captains took a deep breath and spoke simultaneously. "Space. We need more of it.

"These are the voyages of the starship *Endocrine.* Its mission: to cruise around the universe looking for novel predicaments to get into. To search the outskirts of the galaxy . . ."

Here their voices diverged. Capt. Ricardo had recently returned to the original wording: " . . . for areas with less crowding, lower tax rates and better schools."

Simultaneously, Capt. Smirk recited his version: " . . . for classy dames."

They chimed in together on the last line. "To boldly go where nobody wanted to go before!"

2

A Ship Divided

"HAVE YOU RIGGED the Preview feature?" Capt. Ricardo muttered out of the side of his mouth.

"Yes, sir," whispered engineer Georgie LaForgery. "It won't show the past, only the future—some random happening about 50 years from now. It'll look like an equipment malfunction."

They watched the conference table fill up rapidly. Capt. Ricardo had insisted that everyone participate in this meeting, leading Capt. Smirk to protest that the matter wasn't important enough to invite everyone. *Still, he thought it important enough to sleep overnight on the conference table so he'd get a good seat,* Ricardo observed.

There was the usual jockeying for position, and latecomers brought lawn chairs to supplement the meager seating around the table. Members of both crews could sit in either half of the conference room, since it had been declared a demilitarized zone.

Capt. Ricardo stood up. "I hereby call this meeting to order," he announced. "Would the secretary please read the minutes of the last—"

"Mr. Chairman," Smirk interrupted, "I move we dispense with the reading of the minutes from the last meeting."

"Second," Smock chimed in.

Capt. Ricardo frowned. Skipping the reading of the minutes always gave him the jitters that something important would be left out. Still, Smirk had used the proper procedure, and Ricardo had no choice but to follow up.

"All those in favor of omitting the reading of the minutes, signify by saying 'aye'," Ricardo said.

"AYE," came the loud response—much louder, in fact, than if everyone in the room had spoken. Ricardo immediately suspected Smirk and Smock of tampering with the voice vote again. *Should I have Wart shake them down for that "crowd noise" sound-effect device they used once before?* Ricardo wondered. *No, better not. It would get things off to a bad start.*

"Opposed?" Total silence. Ricardo shot a stern glance at Piker to indicate that he should oppose the measure. Piker defiantly stared back at the Captain. Ricardo thought, *What's eating HIM?*

"The motion carries. The secretary will dispense with the reading of the minutes," said Ricardo. Accordingly, Yoohoo flipped her steno pad over to a fresh page and sat with pen poised to take notes.

"Is there any old business?" Ricardo continued.

"Today is Dr. McCaw's birthday," someone said.

"He said *old* business, not *ancient* business," someone else piped up.

"Quiet, please," Ricardo said. "Dr. McCaw's birthday is duly noted for the record. Anything else?"

Dacron raised his hand. "Yes, Mr. Dacron?" said Ricardo.

"Mr. Chairman," said Dacron, "I would like to remind everyone that we need to update our bylaws. You will recall that I have raised this issue during each of the last 57 meetings, and it has always been tabled. Do you think we might—"

Dacron froze in midsentence as Mr. Smock, sitting next to him, made a swift, smooth movement behind the android's back. Dacron collapsed, hitting his head on the table with a loud *thunk*.

Ricardo acknowledged Mr. Smock's contribution with a nod and continued, "All right, let's move on to new business."

"Mr. Chairman." Smirk leapt in immediately. "I move we use the Preview feature of the computer to find my crew's ship before it was destroyed in the battle with the Jargonites."

"Second," said Mr. Smock.

"Any discussion?" asked Ricardo. There was none; everybody was eager to use the Preview feature to look into the past. They were all restless for some good entertainment since there had been nothing decent on television lately.

Ricardo nodded to Georgie, who went to the wall and activated the Preview's viewer-friendly programming screen. Georgie entered the data as prompted:

Stardate: 911.007-3.14
Place: Somewhere off the starboard side of Earth
Precise location/object/building/suite number, etc.:
USS *Endocrine* commanded by James T. Smirk
Collision damage waiver? No

Georgie pressed "Enter" and pretended to wait for the Preview to move backward and show them the time they sought. But the Preview flashed an "Error" message, and a recorded voice stated:

"The year you have entered . . . 911.007-3.14 . . . has been disconnected. We apologize for the inconvenience. For your viewing pleasure, the Preview network provides the following segment of the future."

"What the . . . " Smirk began in dismay.

The Preview screen lit up with the legend "Planet Earth / Maplewood, New Jersey / 50 years in the future."

"This isn't what we wanted," Smirk protested.

The Preview screen showed a crowd milling around inside a convention hall. A banner overhead read "Welcome, Wrekkies."

Smirk forgot about his objection. He and everyone else in the room stared at the screen, astonished—for there in the convention hall were people who looked strangely like the *Endocrine* crew.

They wore *Endocrine* uniforms and Vulture ears and Kringle foreheads and plastic communicator pins. They greeted each other as "Ensign Kilbourn" and "Commander Rexnord" and "Lieutenant Mader." They toured a life-sized replica of the *Endocrine*'s Bridge. And they bought all sorts of items imprinted with the likenesses of *Endocrine* crew-members: framed posters and plastic dolls and refrigerator magnets and bumper stickers and toilet seat covers and lunch boxes and day-of-the-week underwear.

Ricardo was stunned. "Freeze program," he gasped, gripping the table for support.

Georgie flicked a switch, and the Preview screen stopped scanning. It locked onto a close-up of a "Genuine Captain Ricardo Night Light" with a bulb glowing inside a plastic replica of Ricardo's head.

There was a moment of dead silence. Then everyone spoke at once.

"What is it?" "Terrific!" "Are you kidding? This is madness!" "Did you see the Troit Lift-and-Separate Bras they were selling?" "Who are they?" "Can we go there?" "How dare they imitate the Kringle brow furrow! I'll break their necks!"

Ricardo had to pound his gavel for several minutes to restore order. Then he spoke, with an obvious effort to keep his tone calm and measured:

"Any other new business?"

"Mr. Chairman, you can't ignore what we've just seen!" Piker objected.

Capt. Smirk chimed in. "Jean-Lucy, just think of it: Fifty years from now, our crew will be the biggest fad on Earth. Doesn't that excite you?"

"No, it does not," Ricardo replied. "As a matter of fact, it's dreadful to think I might encounter an object like a life-size poster of myself, sometime in the next half-century."

"Huh—you should live so long," muttered Piker.

"What was that?" Ricardo snapped. Piker glowered back at him, refusing to answer. Ricardo continued, "I heard that!"

"Then why'd you ask me what I said?" Piker retorted.

Frustrated, Ricardo slammed down his gavel a half-inch from where Piker's hand rested on the table. "You're out of order, Number One," he growled.

The other crewmembers resumed their argument over whether the scene in the Preview was wonderful or awful. Meanwhile, Georgie began fooling around with the Preview again.

"What are you doing, Lieutenant?" Ricardo demanded.

"I was just curious, Captain," said Georgie, "about what triggered this 'wrekkie' movement. How do these people in the future know so much about us? Maybe I can find out how it all got started."

"Good idea," responded Ricardo. They watched the Preview screen as Georgie scanned backward from the convention. Faster and faster he scanned; his eyes and brain were accustomed to watching lightning-quick images from years of television channel-switching with the remote control. Ricardo, however, began to get dizzy.

"Take it easy, Lieutenant," Ricardo requested. "Make it slow."

Just then Georgie found what he was looking for. "There," he said, bringing the image down to normal speed. Everyone else stopped talking and began to watch along with them.

The Preview flashed the legend "Planet Earth / Residence of Herschel Kinnickinnic / Maplewood, New Jersey / 40 years in the future."

The Preview showed that as the adolescent Herschel sprawled in an easy chair watching "Leave It to Beaver," a blinding flash of light split the room, and the television

There in the convention hall were people who looked strangely like the *Endocrine* crew.

WELCOME WRECKIES
I ♡ DACRON
AUTHORIZED SCALE MODEL
PROGRAM

exploded. As the smoke cleared, Herschel examined the remains of the TV. Next to the shattered picture tube, he found a videotape.

"Uhhhh . . . the time rift," Piker moaned. Ricardo glanced suspiciously at his First Officer.

Herschel took the videotape to his room; it, too, was equipped with a TV and a VCR. He popped the tape into the player and began to watch.

"Hey, that's the tape Westerly Flusher made of us at our work stations," Zulu observed.

"So dat's how dey found out vhat ve're like," Checkout said.

Georgie pressed fast-forward, and the crew watched the future unfold on the Preview screen. Herschel, intrigued by the videotape, watched it several times. Then he invited some friends to view it with him. Soon they were dressing like the *Endocrine* crew and holding monthly meetings. Within a few years, the meetings grew so large that they were taken over by a professional organization, Getalife Conventions.

"Hmmm. Perhaps all we need to do is prevent Westerly from making the videotape, and this whole chain of events will never occur," Ricardo speculated. "But what other consequences might there be?" No one could answer him. Ricardo continued, "Mr. Smock, I'd like to have Mr. Dacron analyze this. Boot him up, will you?"

Smock reached over and flicked Dacron's switch. The android jerked up to a sitting position and chattered, "Positronic Program, Version 5.0, copyright 1992 by MaxiWord Corporation. 989,758,170 bytes total disc space. CONFIG.SYS. CONFIG.BAT. chkdsk c:>\vocab\endless [enter]." He blinked twice, then stated, "Lt. Cmdr. Dacron reporting for duty, sir."

"Dacron, what would happen if we went back in time and prevented Westerly from filming our crew?" asked Capt. Ricardo.

"There is a 99 percent probability that our current time-

The android jerked up to a sitting position and chattered.

line would be affected," Dacron responded. "Without the videotape, Westerly would not have been accepted into the Starfreak Academy Film School. Instead, he would still be here on the *Endocrine.*"

Capt. Ricardo grimaced. "Well, so much for *that* idea," he concluded. "It looks like we're going to have to go forward 40 years and prevent Herschel from finding the videotape."

"Sir." Piker stood up and cocked his head, preparing to make a dramatic statement. "What about your longstanding objection to altering the space/time continuum?"

Ricardo, wondering again why his First Officer seemed to have a bug in his britches, decided to assert his authority. He told Piker, "I'm entitled to change my policy. As the saying goes, 'A foolish consistency is the hobgoblin of little minds'—a phenomenon that's undoubtedly very familiar to you, Number One."

Piker, suspecting he'd been insulted but not sure just how, sat down and mulled over possible retorts.

Capt. Smirk spoke up. "If we're going forward, it should be to *encourage* Herschel to make this wrekkie thing even bigger and better. Why, if we play our cards right, we could be big, really big—more popular than the Beatles, even."

A gasp of dismay escaped Mr. Smock's lips.

"Come on, Smock," Smirk continued. "I know you like your privacy and all that, but this fan worship could be a lot of fun once you get into it."

Mr. Smock shuddered.

"I'm with Captain Ricardo," stated co-engineer Snot. "We ought ta go forward 'n' get the tape before it falls into the hands of this Herschel lad."

"Nyet!" shouted Checkout, jumping to his feet. "Ve should go help Herschel. Ve can make personal appearances, sign autographs, and endorse more products!"

"Siddown, you little twerp!" snarled Dr. McCaw. "What in heaven's name is so great about having our picture stamped on a toilet seat cover?"

"Don't tell him to sit down, you big bully," snapped Dr. Flusher, reaching into her pocket for a scalpel to fling at McCaw.

The argument among the crew regained its momentum. A few people squared off for a fistfight, and security chief Wart picked up a chair to throw. Capt. Ricardo, envisioning another window being broken and more valuable furnishings destroyed, shouted above the din:

"All right, all right! We'll vote on it!"

Everybody quieted down. After the room fell silent, Piker abruptly blurted to Capt. Ricardo, "I'll let it go this time, but if you call me a hobgoblin again I'm going to file a grievance with the First Officers' Union Local 2598."

Capt. Ricardo stared at Piker for a long moment, then shook his head and returned his attention to the matter of voting. Ricardo decided to poll for individual opinions, since he was afraid an ordinary voice vote would allow Smirk to use his crowd noise sound-effect device to sway the outcome again.

"The issue we're voting on is whether or not to let this 'wrekkie' phenomenon occur," said Ricardo. "Should we allow Herschel to find the videotape? Please confine yourselves to a short statement."

They went around the table counterclockwise. Piker, seated at Ricardo's right, was first.

"I say yes," Piker stated, "because I think we're entitled to a few positive strokes, and these people would obviously worship the ground we walk on."

Dr. McCaw was next. "Rubbish!" he grizzled. "I'm a doctor, not a superstar!"

"I have no feelings about the matter, either negative or positive," said Dacron, "for I am an android, and as you know, androids cannot feel emotion, and—" *Thunk.* Dacron collapsed onto the table again.

Mr. Smock smoothly slid his arm from behind Dacron's back and folded his hands in front of him. "I agree with Capt. Ricardo that we should forestall this phenomenon," he said, "since it disturbs me to see the noble Vulture ear being worn by outsiders."

Checkout said, "I say we inwestigate dese fans; dis is the first time in my life anyvone has ewer looked up to me."

Zulu shrugged. "I don't see what all the fuss is about either way."

"Ditto," echoed Georgie.

"You've never been laid off," countered Dr. Flusher. "Ever since Starfreak yanked me away from the *Endocrine* and then sent me back, I've been looking for some perks to make up for it. This fan worship could be just what the doctor ordered."

"I'd love to sing to the fans," Yoohoo trilled.

"That's reason enough for me to sit tight, right here in the present," Guano grumbled.

Deanna Troit looked troubled. "They're hiding something," she judged. "I'm reading multiple personalities in each one of them. I don't think we should interfere."

"I'm agin' it," said Mr. Snot. "They'd probably be wantin' me to explain warped drive to 'em. I say we put a stop to the whole thing."

"I agree," snarled Wart. "We should launch an immediate attack on the convention hall."

"Mr. Wart," said Smirk in a mildly reproving tone, "you'd attack? With so many charming ladies there? I think this is wonderful. In fact, I'd rather go to the future and attend this convention than go to the past and get our ship. I say aye, aye, a thousand times aye!"

Now that everyone else had spoken, Capt. Ricardo made his statement. "For the record, my official stand is 'Bah, humbug.' " He made sure Yoohoo dutifully recorded this in the minutes.

With the discussion safely behind them, Smock reached over and turned Dacron back on.

"Will the secretary please report the tally?" Ricardo

grumbled. He didn't like the way all of this was shaping up.

"The official vote," said Yoohoo, "on the question of whether to allow Herschel to find the videotape is five 'pro,' five 'con,' and five neutral."

"It's a tie, so we can do whatever we want," Smirk swiftly asserted. "All you Pros, gather round." He stood on his chair and motioned for them to come. Piker, Yoohoo, Beverage Flusher and Checkout moved toward him.

"All Cons, assemble now to fight for the glorious cause!" shouted Wart, raising his fist. "Let your blood run hot in this day of the warrior. This Herschel must be crushed."

"Just a minute . . . " murmured Ricardo, who counted himself among the Cons but didn't appreciate being treated like a foster Kringle. Nevertheless, as Smock, McCaw and Snot gathered around Wart, Ricardo joined them.

The remaining five, backing away from the newly-forming groups, found themselves assembling into a third group of their own. "Well, here we are," observed Deanna Troit, "the Neutrals."

"Hey, let's hear it for the Neuts!" said Georgie in his bounciest cheerleader voice. Deanna, Dacron, Guano and Zulu stared at him, and he mumbled sheepishly, "Uh, maybe not."

The Pros and the Cons huddled in separate corners discussing their plans, but with Wart's booming voice within the Cons, and Piker's random dramatic statements for the Pros, they soon overheard each other. The Cons were figuring out how to build a time machine to go forward and prevent Herschel from viewing the videotape. The Pros wanted to reach the same point, thwart the Cons, and encourage Herschel.

All ten of them realized at the same instant that it was just a matter of who got there first with a time machine. They all raced for the door and charged through at once, somehow managing to get everyone stuck in a clump of torsos, arms and legs.

Dacron shrugged and walked over to the entrance. He gave the whole pack of them a quick shove through the doorway and into the future.

3

Déjà Boo-Boo

"YOU WANT *ME* to build our time machine?" Piker repeated.

"That's what I said, Commander," Smirk told him. "Do you have a problem with that?"

"Well, sir," Piker said, "the job seems more appropriate for one of the subordinates, don't you think? I sort of pictured them doing the hands-on work while you and I would sit back and, uh, you know—command."

"Commander Piker." Smirk lowered his voice and indicated the rest of their team, seated at an adjacent table in Ten-Foreplay. "Which one of them is capable of building it? Beverage Flusher? Yoohoo? *Checkout?*"

"Yes, but my job description normally wouldn't cover that sort of . . ." Piker continued. Smirk held up a hand to silence him.

"I expect my right-hand man to roll up his sleeves, move to the firing line, play hardball, roll with the punches, fight in the trenches, and whistle while he works," Smirk insisted. "Is that clear, Commander?"

Piker nodded.

"After all," Smirk went on, "when we were stranded on Earth during that Keebler episode, Mr. Smock rigged up a short-wave radio transmitter out of egg cartons and aluminum foil. That's the kind of practical help I need."

"Yes, sir." Piker mulled over the problem as he left Ten-Foreplay. He realized this could be his golden opportunity to impress Capt. Smirk. Perhaps Smirk would even hire him as First Officer now that Mr. Smock had joined the Cons.

Soon Piker was lost in thought—without a map, as usual. *How am I going to build a time machine? Do they print blueprints for them in* Popular Mechanix? *Maybe we should try to rent one instead. Captain Smirk mentioned something about Smock building stuff out of egg cartons. What's an egg carton?*

Piker wandered into his room and flicked on the television, hoping the alpha waves would stimulate his imagination. By coincidence, his favorite science fiction program, "Dr. Whom," was underway. Dr. Whom had just finished knitting an extra two feet onto his muffler and was about to step into his time machine, the Tardy.

"That's it," Piker concluded. "I'll build a Tardy."

Later that day, Piker summoned his fellow Pros with the news that their time machine was assembled and ready for travel. The contraption stood covered with a tarp in the middle of the workshop. When everyone had gathered around it, Piker unveiled the machine with a flourish and announced, "Ta-daaa!" The other Pros stared at it for a long time.

Finally Checkout said flatly, "I don't get it."

"It looks like an old phone booth or something," Beverage ventured.

"A time machine can look like a phone booth," Piker retorted. "Haven't any of you ever seen the one on 'Dr. Whom'?"

"I've never watched that program," said Yoohoo. "It's on at the same time as 'Quilting with Gladys.' And I never miss 'Quilting with Gladys.' "

"Well, take my word for it. It's a time machine," said Piker, irritated at their lack of enthusiasm.

"Let's get going," Capt. Smirk urged them. "We want to make sure we reach Herschel before the Cons do. So, Commander, how does this machine work? Do we each take turns using it?"

"Uh, no," Piker answered. "We all have to get in at once."

Beverage hooted. "You want all five of us to cram into this little phone booth?"

"Captain, I'm frightened," Yoohoo quavered.

"Let's stay calm, everyone," Smirk said. "It's just for a moment, and then we'll be out." Gently he herded them into the booth. As he passed Piker, Smirk muttered, "I hope you know what you're doing."

Piker hoped so, too. He pushed Smirk's shoulder, forcing it past the doorway, then squeezed himself inside and shut the door. The five of them were packed solid.

"Ugh! Who had onions for lunch?" Yoohoo demanded. She wriggled her hand free and waved it in front of her nose.

"Excuse me, excuse me," Piker said, pushing his way toward the telephone. "I have to dial this thing to get us where we're going." Awkwardly they reshuffled themselves until Piker could reach the phone. He dialed a dozen digits and waited.

In a moment the Tardy was surrounded by darkness. "I think we've arrived," Piker said.

Smirk forced the door open and stepped out. They had landed in an open field, and it was apparently late at night. The others crept out after Smirk.

"This doesn't look like Maplewood, New Jersey," Beverage observed.

"Shhhh!" Smirk ordered. "I see someone up ahead!"

Their eyes adjusted to the darkness; they could make out the vague outlines of several people moving to and fro. Smirk dropped to his hands and knees; he crept toward the mysterious figures, motioning that the others should follow.

As her companions crawled through the grass, Yoohoo

The five of them were packed solid.

hesitated, certain that the rough terrain would put a run in her pantyhose. She loped forward on her hands and feet, trying to keep her knees off the ground. The awkward position forced her to look down rather than ahead, so she didn't notice when Checkout stopped just in front of her. Yoohoo butted Checkout with her head.

"Ooof!" exclaimed Checkout. "Vat da heck—"

"Shhhh!" Smirk told them; but it was too late.

"Who's thar?" demanded one of the figures up ahead. "Soldiers, see to that noise yonder!"

A moment later, Smirk and his companions were surrounded, with a thicket of rifles aimed at their heads.

"Nice going, Commander," Smirk muttered. The five Pros sat on the ground in the midst of a military encampment. From the conversations going on around them, they had deduced that Piker's time machine had brought them to Fort Sumter on the eve of the outbreak of the Civil War.

"I don't understand it," Piker mumbled, shaking his head in disbelief. "I must have dialed the wrong number."

"Wrong number!" Smirk hissed. "You were supposed to move us to the future, not the past! How could you be so far off?"

"Captain, I'm frightened," Yoohoo bleated.

"Quiet, Yankee spies!" ordered one of the guards standing over them.

Capt. Smirk fidgeted. It made him nervous to sit here under the Confederate guards' control, with the Tardy hidden somewhere in the darkness between them and the fort.

Yet in the midst of his uneasiness, something puzzled him. According to his calculations, the Confederates should be preparing to attack Fort Sumter at dawn, triggering the first official battle of the war. But for some reason, in this timeline, the Confederates were talking about negotiations. It almost sounded like they were ready to make concessions to the Union.

Smirk and his companions were surrounded.

Maybe war can be avoided, Smirk thought. *No Civil War . . .*

His mind reeled with the implications. If there were no Civil War, many lives could be spared . . . an entire publishing genre would never exist . . . and "Ashokan Farewell" wouldn't make the Top Ten.

But Smirk knew these issues were still up in the air. The important thing right now was for the five of them to get out of this timeline. He came up with a plan and whispered it to Piker; Piker nodded and, using whispers and gestures, communicated the message to the others.

Smirk felt a moment's satisfaction. *There's one thing you can say about Piker—he knows how to take orders,* Smirk thought. *Smock would have argued that my plan is foolhardy and dangerous. And it is, but so what? Piker's like me, an action kind of guy. Maybe I should create a position for him on my permanent staff.*

Smirk's strategy was for the Pros to stun the guards with their phasers, which the soldiers hadn't confiscated since they didn't recognize them as weapons. Then Smirk would hold off the remaining troops while his companions dashed to the Tardy. He would join them last, keeping the soldiers at bay with his phaser as he boarded the time machine.

The only drawback was that they'd need to perfectly coordinate their dash to the Tardy. If anyone's timing was off . . .

Smirk shook his head; it was too late for second thoughts. Dawn would break soon. This was the time to make their move.

The others watched for his signal. "To your marks . . . " Smirk whispered. "Set . . . go!"

They all rose at once and fired at the guards, knocking them unconscious.

Smirk pointed his phaser at the remaining soldiers, who backed away warily. "Make a break for it!" Smirk shouted to his companions.

They scrambled away—in all directions. In the darkness and confusion, it was hard even to see one another, much less the Tardy way out in the field. Yoohoo and Beverage ran smack into a supply tent. Checkout tripped over a campfire. Piker sprinted ahead of the soldiers' front line, then collided with a tree.

Smirk despaired. *How am I supposed to cover for them when they're running around like chickens with their heads cut off?*

The commotion attracted the attention of a commander stationed next to the cannon. He pointed straight ahead at Piker. "The Yankee spies are escaping! Fire!" the commander ordered.

The cannon blasted—and, since it was pointed at Fort Sumter, incidentally began the Civil War.

Bored Silly

"WHAT IS THAT thing, Snot—a carnival funhouse? I can't time travel in that. I'm a doctor, not a carny worker," McCaw groused.

Mr. Snot frowned. "Forrr pity's sake," he answered, "haven't ye ever seen the old 'Time Funnel' television series, mon? They used to travel back in time wi' a spinnin' tunnel just like this one. The rest o' the equipment just happened to be attached to the tunnel, that's all."

The Cons stood inspecting Mr. Snot's just-unveiled time machine at the same moment Piker was misdialing the Pros into the past. Neither group knew what the others were up to.

Snot's time machine did look like a carnival funhouse. Its entrance was a large spinning barrel painted with stripes. Beyond that were steps that rocked back and forth in alternating directions, as well as some warped mirrors.

Wart kicked the side of the structure, testing its strength. "Hmmmph," he grunted. "You got this from the HolidayDeck, didn't you? It sounds hollow."

"And what if I did?" Snot retorted. "It isn't easy to find parts for such a—"

"Never mind, Mr. Snot," said Capt. Ricardo. "Is the time machine ready to use?"

"Aye, sir," replied Snot. "As soon as we've all gotten to

the control room inside, I'll send us off."

Mr. Smock went first. After studying the spinning barrel for a moment and calculating the rate of spin and various tangents of trajectory, he managed to stay upright while negotiating his way to the other side.

He made it look so easy that the others, following him, were caught off guard and lost their footing. Ricardo wobbled, grabbing Wart for support; but the Kringle was already unsteady, and he crashed into Snot, who in turn fell against McCaw. Down they all went, rolling around like rocks in a cement mixer. Finally they rolled to the other side and spilled out at Smock's feet.

Next they climbed the shifting steps, with varying degrees of success. Smock and Wart moved up fairly easily, but Ricardo, Snot and McCaw had to cling to a side railing and drag themselves up.

Panting and sweating, they followed the funhouse maze to the next room, which was filled with mirrors. Mr. Smock had gotten there first, and he was studying the mirrors in puzzlement. "I fail to understand the purpose of these distorted images," he stated.

McCaw muttered, "I always thought these funhouse mirrors were pretty stupid."

"They're supposed to be funny, Mr. Smock," Ricardo said. "See? When you stand in front of this one, it makes you look extraordinarily tall and thin. Whereas the image of the one where Wart is standing is all wavy. And Snot's reflection is distorted to look grossly overweight."

McCaw stepped beside Snot and studied his own image in the same mirror. "No, it's not distorted," he observed. "This is an ordinary mirror. That's Snot's real reflection." He guffawed. "Now, *that's* funny!" Ricardo, realizing that he'd unintentionally insulted Snot, blushed until his entire skull resembled a GE Intimate Moments pink light bulb.

Snot, muttering angrily under his breath, stomped over to the control panel just beyond the mirrored room. He set the controls and announced, "Here we go."

Panting and sweating, they followed the funhouse maze to the next room.

The funhouse shook and rattled for a minute; then the motion stopped. "I think we're there," Snot said.

The Cons made their way back down the steps and through the barrel. As they spilled out of the time machine, everyone realized that something was very wrong. This was definitely not New Jersey.

A mechanical arm reached out, grabbed Smock by the ear, and lifted him several inches off the ground. The arm belonged to a half-human, half-machine creature which examined Smock impartially. With its pasty white skin and cluttered mechanical body parts, the creature looked like a hybrid between Dacron and the props department of the movie *Brazil.*

"Don't struggle, Mr. Smock!" Ricardo urged.

Within moments, more of these creatures arrived and began hauling the other Cons to their feet.

"What the devil are they?" asked McCaw.

Capt. Ricardo, his voice filled with dread, answered, "The Bored."

An hour later, the five Cons shivered in a holding pen. The Bored had stashed them there after stripping them to their underwear and sending in a mechanical tailor to measure them for new limbs.

The Cons had managed to figure out that they were being held prisoner in a Bored ship. They also knew that they'd gone way too far into the future—even farther than during Starfreak's first encounter with the Bored—since the aliens had undergone minor design changes like the addition of stereo headphones and chest-front ice dispensers.

"Perhaps if you can recall more about your previous interactions with the Bored, Captain, it will help us escape from them now," said Mr. Smock.

"I've told you all I remember, Mr. Smock," said Ricardo wearily. "They kidnapped me from the *Endocrine,* turned me into a Bored named Lowcutie, and made me a pawn in their takeover of the universe."

Ricardo fervently hoped that Smock would mellow out soon. The Captain was bone-tired from the unaccustomed stress of coping with a right-hand man with a brain. If Piker were here, he would have run out of dramatic statements long ago and probably would be napping by now.

But Mr. Smock persisted in analyzing the situation. "This ship we are trapped in—how is it constructed?"

Wart answered him. "On the outside, a Bored ship looks like a Radio Shack outlet that has been crushed in a trash compactor. Here in the interior, all the Bored creatures are interchangeable units connected to a central power source. They have multiple redundant layers that are impossible to penetrate."

"Kind of like the bureaucracy of Starfreak Command, eh?" cracked McCaw.

"Exactly how did they turn you into a Bored?" Smock asked the Captain.

Ricardo sighed. "Mr. Smock, is this really necessary?"

"The details might suggest an escape strategy," Smock replied.

"Oh, all right," Ricardo conceded. "They grafted mechanical parts onto my body. I got a laser-beam eye, a stainless steel pancreas, a forearm/hand unit that doubled as a can opener, and, uh . . . other enhancements."

"What other enhancements?" Smock insisted.

"Well . . . " Ricardo hesitated, then leaned over and whispered something into Smock's ear.

Smock raised a Vulture eyebrow in surprise. "I see," he said evenly. "And after you were rescued, all these alterations were returned to normal human form?"

"Yes. I had Dr. Flusher surgically remove the Bored parts and send them back," said Ricardo, squirming a little under Smock's gaze. "Uh, that is, all except the . . . you know."

Smock's eyebrow rose higher.

"They kidnapped me from the *Endocrine* and turned me into a Bored named Lowcutie."

"Well, I thought that might come in handy sometime," Ricardo defended himself.

"So far, this information has not suggested how we could escape," Smock said. "Mr. Wart, you were on board this ship also. Perhaps you can tell us something more."

Wart thought for a moment, then answered, "There is one other thing. On our first rescue mission, we discovered Capt. Ricardo's discarded uniform in a refrigerator vegetable drawer. That seemed unusual."

"Did you take it with you?" Smock asked.

"No. We left it in the drawer," replied the Kringle. Then his eyes glimmered as he realized the significance of Smock's question. "That means it may still be here . . . "

Smock nodded as he completed the thought: " . . . With a communicator pin attached, we hope."

As soon as the Cons realized that Ricardo's communicator pin was stashed in some forgotten cranny of the Bored ship, offering them a means of calling for help, they all pitched in at what they did best: arguing.

Each of the five crabby pessimists made his own unique contribution to the squabble. Ricardo overanalyzed their options and called for a vote, irritating Wart, Snot and McCaw. Then Smock pointed out the futility of anger in the situation, which only heightened their irritation.

McCaw vetoed the initial escape plan—"I'm a doctor, not Houdini." Snot pointed out that the mechanics of the plan were unsound and predicted they'd all be "blown into wee bits of flotsam and jetsam" if they tried to beam out. Wart proposed a strategy involving maximum mayhem, and everyone ignored his idea, just as they'd done to every mouthwateringly violent proposal he'd ever made since joining the crew.

Finally, the sheer discomfort of sitting around shivering in their underwear forced them out of the holding pen to search the ship. The Bored hadn't left them with much clothing. Ricardo wore boxer shorts imprinted with the coat-of-arms pattern of his alma mater, the Stuffordshire Boys' School. Snot had an old-fashioned sleeveless t-shirt and an underkilt. Smock's jockey shorts were ultramodern, with an energy-efficient Velcro fly. Dr. McCaw's underwear was blue standard-issue surgical garb he'd "borrowed" from Sick Bay. And Wart wore leather briefs accented with metal studs.

They crept down the corridor, wondering how to locate Ricardo's old uniform. A major clue emerged when McCaw spotted a Building Directory/Floor Plan on the wall. They plotted a route from the "you are here" dot to the Pantry area in Corridor 1179D.

On the way there, they passed the room where their time machine had come to rest. Several Bored were dismantling it and tossing the parts into a recycling bin. Without weapons there was nothing the Cons could do to stop them, so they continued their search.

When they reached the Pantry, Wart immediately recognized the vegetable drawer. Ricardo's uniform lay inside, with its communicator pin still in working order.

Ricardo flicked it on. "*Endocrine,* this is Capt. Ricardo. Come in." There was no response. "I'm sure they're receiving the signal," Ricardo said. "*Endocrine,* please respond."

A metallic voice crackled to life behind them: "Lowcutie!" Whirling around, they saw that a dozen Bored were advancing into the Pantry.

"Lowcutie," said the twelve Bored, speaking with one voice, "you have failed to return a particularly valuable body part grafted onto you during a previous visit. You must surrender it immediately."

5

Neuts to the Rescue

"AAAAAAAAAAAAAAAAAAA!"

Capt. Ricardo's scream traveled through time and emerged through the "hey, you" speakers on the *Endocrine*'s Bridge. It was a dramatic scream, almost Shakespearean in its masterful tone and timbre. But ultimately it did not make a sound on the Bridge, for there was no one there to hear it.

Left on their own, the Neuts—the *Endocrine* officers who hadn't backed either time-travel scheme—had stretched the art of goofing off to new heights. They figured, why bother with tedious chores like charting new planets or running a Class II diagnostic on the snack dispensers when there was a strong possibility that the Pros or Cons would screw up the timeline and it would all simply cease to exist?

At the moment, the Neuts were lounging around in Ten-Foreplay.

Dacron stood at the far end of the bar wearing a cowboy hat. He loved pretending Ten-Foreplay was a Wild West saloon. "Barkeep!" he called. "Another round of simpahol drafts for us cowpokes. It has been a long, dusty trail ride herding them doggies from Houston to Alamogordo."

"Don't you think you've had enough, Dacron?" asked Guano, folding her arms across her chest. Unlike the oth-

The Neuts were lounging around in Ten-Foreplay.

ers, who could shake off the effects of the synthetic alcohol substitute, Dacron had never gotten the hang of it. The simpahol jazzed up his circuits for hours.

"Enough? What is 'enough'?" Dacron asked, extending his hand in a stagey gesture. "It is said that it is better to give than to receive, but how much giving is enough, and how much receiving is too much? And it is also said that too often we love things and use people, when we should use things and love people, but in reality it is people and not things that cause all the misery in the galaxy. After all, when was the last time a 'thing' hijacked a starship, or stepped on someone's foot, or . . ."

"Guano, would you give him the beer already?" Georgie whined. "The faster he drinks, the sooner he'll move out of this blabby stage and into his laughing jag."

"Oh, all right. Here, cowboy." Guano drew a simpahol beer from the tap.

Dacron grinned. "Please be sure to slide it down the bar in the traditional Western manner," he requested.

Guano shoved the mug toward Dacron from her end of the counter. The mug slid past Dacron, flew off the edge of the bar, and crashed on the floor. Two seconds later, Dacron made a delayed grab for it. He stared at the shattered mug at his feet, then turned to Guano. "May we try that again, please?" he asked. Guano began drawing another beer.

Meanwhile, Zulu sat at one of the tables, swatting his paddle ball. "I wonder what the Pros and Cons are doing right now?" he remarked.

"Ask me if I care," Troit snapped. "Probably off setting a new record for making and breaking commitments." She pulled out a voodoo doll and placed it on the table. Its face looked remarkably like Capt. Smirk's. Next she held up a pin and studied the doll, choosing a tender spot in which to stick it.

Guano looked uneasy. "Deanna, this voodoo stuff gives me the creeps. Haven't you gotten over Capt. Smirk yet?

Sure, he broke your engagement, but I thought you'd adjust pretty quick, being a counselor and all."

"This is a very healthy outlet for my hostility," Troit said through clenched teeth. She stuck the pin into the doll's shoulder.

"Well, I shay good riddance to all of them," Dacron slurred, leaning on the bar, "particularly Mr. Schmock. I am not sure why, but whenever he is nearby I develop a headache."

"Headache . . . heartache . . . pain in the butt," Troit muttered, pulling the pin out of the doll's shoulder and plunging it into its head, then its chest, then its rear end.

"Shay, hash anybody heard the one about the rabbi, the priesht and the minishter?" Dacron asked.

"Here we go," observed Georgie. "Dacron's entering his laughing phase."

"We'd better get him out of here," Zulu said. "Remember what happened last time? He kept doing that stand-up routine until he started hemorrhaging. I think he calms down a lot faster when he's off by himself."

"Let's take him to the Bridge," Georgie suggested.

"A priesht, a rabbi and a minishter are shtranded in a shufflecraft," Dacron continued, "trying to figure out how to call for help . . . " Dacron kept on babbling as Zulu and Georgie swooped him up from either side, carrying him out of Ten-Foreplay and into the Crewmover.

" . . . And the minister says, 'This is the 24th century. God does not exist anymore!' " Dacron delivered the punchline and dissolved in whoops of helpless laughter just as Georgie and Zulu carried him onto the Bridge from the Crewmover, the *Endocrine*'s horizontal/vertical elevator to all parts of the ship. Plopping him into the captain's chair, they left the Bridge and returned to Ten-Foreplay.

As his laughter began to subside about half an hour later, Dacron began looking for a new diversion. Still giggling, he pulled out the latest issue of *Playdroid* magazine and studied the foldout of a fully functional female. Then he remembered that it was late afternoon and "All My Androids" was about to come on. He switched the View-screen to its TV setting and cranked up the footrest on the Captain's chair.

He discovered it was still a little early; the broadcast of "The Bald and the Beautiful" wasn't over yet. Dacron had never been able to get into that show, though he knew it was Capt. Ricardo's favorite. He turned down the sound to wait for his program to begin.

In the sudden silence on the Bridge, Dacron heard a faint voice. "Helllllp . . . hellllllp . . . " It seemed to be coming from the "hey, you" speakers. He cranked up the volume on the receiver.

"Hello?" Dacron inquired.

"Dacron, is that you?" It was Capt. Ricardo.

"Unnhhh," Dacron moaned. Dimly he recalled talking to Capt. Ricardo on the "hey, you" frequency a while ago. The conversation had seemed so important at the time. But now it took all of Dacron's concentration just to raise his head gingerly from the conference room table, rub his temples, then let his head flop back down amid the glasses of Alka-Seltzer, bottles of aspirin and mugs of hot coffee. "Unnnhhhhh."

"Well, this certainly is one of the more entertaining staff meetings I've ever attended," Georgie remarked.

"It sure beats following Robert's Rules of Order," Zulu noted.

"Dacron," Deanna said, "when you called this meeting, you said it was an emergency. Can you just tell us what Capt. Ricardo and the Cons need, so we can help them?"

Dacron turned his face to one side so that his mouth no longer pressed against the table. Without lifting his head, he moaned, "They went too far into the future. They are trapped in the Bored ship. We will have to build a time machine to rescue them. I swear I am going to die."

"Are they in any immediate danger?" Zulu asked.

"Capt. Ricardo is at great financial risk," Dacron said. "The Bored may confiscate his heirlooms."

"His heirlooms? Dacron, what are you talking about?" Georgie demanded.

Dacron explained, "He said if we do not arrive soon, he will lose the family jewels."

The four subordinate Neuts sat on the Bridge discussing what to do next. Dacron, their leader, had ended the meeting by announcing that he would not allow the effects of the simpahol to interfere with the performance of his duties. He'd lifted his head, opened his eyes, and with great dignity, crawled out of the conference room. He'd made it as far as the doorway, where he now lay, sleeping it off.

"Let's face it—only Dacron can build a time machine," Georgie pointed out.

"Why can't you do it?" asked Zulu. "You're an engineer."

"I never studied Time Mechanics," Georgie admitted. "It wasn't a required course, so I skipped it and took Intro to Yoga instead."

"Maybe we should try to contact Capt. Smirk and the Pros," Guano suggested. "We haven't heard from them lately, either."

Georgie agreed. From the communicator panel at the Tactical station, he sent out a signal and began zeroing in on the Pros' location.

"Where are they? Did they make it to the correct place and time?" Zulu asked.

"I don't think the time is right," Georgie said, studying the readouts. "As a matter of fact, I think they're in the past. As for where they are, it seems to be a Class M&M planet."

"You know, I never understood what a Class M&M planet is," Guano mused.

"That means it's capable of supporting human life, with

a breathable atmosphere and a hospitable climate," Georgie explained.

Guano looked puzzled. "Aren't they all like that?" she asked. "I mean, when was the last time you guys put on space suits or helmets when beaming down to the surface of an unfamiliar planet?"

"Hey, I think I've reached them," Georgie said. "Hello? This is Lt. Georgie LaForgery of the USS *Endocrine*. Who's there?"

"Smirk here," came the voice. "What can we do for you, Lieutenant?"

"When and where did you land, Capt. Smirk?"

"We're on Earth, at Fort Sumter," Smirk said breezily, "and the time is—oh, 1860-ish."

"Fort Sumter . . ." Georgie repeated in amazement. " . . . during the Civil War . . . Are you and the other Pros all right, Captain? I hear cannons in the background."

"Oh, there's a bit of a skirmish going on at the moment, but we're fine, Lieutenant—"

"No, we're not!" Piker's voice interrupted. "He's just too proud to ask for help. Georgie, get us out of here! We're trapped—"

His voice halted abruptly, and Capt. Smirk came back on the audio channel. "Actually, it *is* getting rather boring here, and we have a slight malfunction in our time machine. If you would be so good as to swing by and pick us up, we'd appreciate it."

"We'll try, Captain," said Georgie, "but first Dacron has to build a time machine, and then we have to rescue the Cons. They're stuck, too. After that, we'll come get you."

Beverage Flusher's voice came over the audio. "Please hurry, Georgie," she said. "Capt. Smirk is having medical problems, and I need to get him to Sick Bay and perform some tests. It's a condition I've never seen before, creating stabbing pains all over his body."

The Neuts turned to look at Troit, who pulled out her voodoo doll and gazed at it with new respect.

"We'll be waiting for you—eeeek!" Flusher's voice was drowned out by a hail of gunfire. The Neuts were puzzled momentarily; then they shrugged it off, and Georgie closed the audio channel.

Early the next morning, Dacron started working on the Neuts' time machine. During the night he'd had his fluids changed and had attended his first meeting of Androids Anonymous. Now he felt like a new pseudo-man.

It took him only a few hours to build the contraption. He applied the latest Japanese quality-control techniques and came up with a just-in-time machine.

Dacron time-traveled to the Bored ship. He found the Cons huddled in a corner, helplessly watching the Bored strip down their funhouse time machine. A frustrated Mr. Smock fiddled with Capt. Ricardo's communicator, which the Bored had disabled immediately after Ricardo's distress call to Dacron. Smock had hoped to fix it and beam them out of there, but it was a hopeless task since he had neither tools nor egg cartons to work with.

The Bored were caught off guard by Dacron's sudden arrival. As the aliens moved to counter this unexpected threat, the Cons made a run for it.

In an instant, Dacron activated a control on the wall panel, disabling the shields that the Bored had placed around the funhouse. Immediately the Neuts locked on to the funhouse and beamed it back to the *Endocrine.* Then Dacron ran down the corridor to catch up with the Cons, with the Bored pursuing just inches behind him.

The Cons had taken advantage of their brief head start to duck into a supply closet. Failing to notice their evasive maneuver, Dacron was about to run past the closet when Wart reached out, grabbed him, pulled him into the closet, and slammed the door shut behind them. The Bored pounded on it furiously.

Everyone but Dacron panted in exhaustion. Finally, between gasps for air, Dr. McCaw blurted out to Dacron,

"Well . . . how are you . . . going to . . . get us out of here . . . Whitey?"

"I was able to beam your funhouse back to the *Endocrine,*" Dacron said, "but we cannot use the transporter ourselves. We must travel in my just-in-time machine. Unfortunately, the Bored are now positioned between us and the machine. Mr. Smock, I will need your help with a procedure enabling me to access their collective consciousness, using my body as a communication channel. That will overcome their resistance, as well as allowing me to pursue my hobby of speaking in funny voices."

Smock stepped forward. "What should I do?" he asked.

Dacron walked over to the intercom unit on the wall, one of hundreds placed throughout the ship to allow two-way communication and play background music. At the moment, its small speaker was broadcasting heavy metal.

On the face of the intercom were buttons marked "Kitchen," "Playroom" and "Nursery." Next to them was a small outlet labeled "AC/DC." Dacron opened the outlet, revealing a tangle of wires.

"This is the conduit for Alien Communication/Direct Connection," Dacron explained to Smock. "You will need to hook up my brain to this outlet." He touched the back of his head. "Here, just beneath my cowlick, is the panel which allows access to my higher functions."

"Do you wish to remain conscious during this procedure, Mr. Dacron?" Smock asked.

Dacron nodded. "It is vital that I stay alert so that I can relay instructions to the Bored."

"Will it hurt?" Smock asked.

"No, it will not."

"Darn," Smock said dryly. He pressed the latch, and the panel to Dacron's brain popped open. "All right, now what do I do?" Smock asked.

"There is a cord there," Dacron told him. "It consists of three intertwined wires, sheathed in black, green, and white plastic, respectively. Do you see it?"

"Yes," Smock answered.

"Pull out the cord," Dacron continued, "separate the wires, and connect the white wire from my brain to the white wire in the receptacle. Please check carefully before connecting. It is vital that you connect white to white."

Smock studied the three wires. The other Cons, standing behind Dacron's back, realized that Smock was considering various options besides white-to-white. McCaw and Snot snickered, and Wart rubbed his hands in anticipation. Only Capt. Ricardo ignored the scene; he looked uncharacteristically distracted, staring straight ahead and babbling soundlessly to himself.

Finally Smock made up his mind. He extended Dacron's white wire and deliberately hooked it to the green wire in the intercom.

Dacron's eyes rolled upward, and his hair frizzed out in all directions, crackling with static electricity. The signal from the intercom snapped his reflexes into the posture of a strutting rock performer: he mimed playing an electric guitar while screaming along with the heavy metal song on the intercom.

McCaw and Snot laughed and laughed till they had to hold their sides; tears ran down their cheeks. Wart strained to keep from cracking an unKringlelike smile, but his eyes twinkled with delight.

Finally Smock decided they'd all had enough fun for one day. He removed the green wire and correctly connected white to white.

Instantly Dacron's expression went blank as he became a conduit for the collective Bored consciousness. The Bored sensed the connection with an unknown entity. They took over Dacron's own vocal mechanism to speak to him, stating in a metallic drone, "Hey there . . . big boy . . . we may be compatible. State your modem."

Dacron switched to his usual tone of voice and countered, "Give me a 'C' prompt." His eyes rolled randomly until the Bored complied. He ordered, "Delete C/BORED/

.." Then Dacron went limp, and Smock disconnected him from the intercom.

As soon as Smock closed Dacron's brain panel, the android regained normal functioning. "I have disabled the Bored," he announced. "They will no longer prevent us from reaching my time machine." Sure enough, out in the hallway the Bored were sprawled around like so many auto parts at the junkyard.

Within moments Dacron got the Cons aboard the just-in-time machine and flew them back to the *Endocrine*'s shuttlebay. The other Neuts had gathered to greet them, and they were surprised when the Cons stepped out of the vehicle in their underwear.

Only Capt. Ricardo was fully dressed, wearing the old uniform he'd reclaimed from the Bored. Georgie approached him, noticing his stunned expression. "Are you all right, Captain?" Georgie asked.

Smock explained, "The Captain is adjusting quite well. His original human parts are now *all* back in place."

Capt. Ricardo's mouth moved, but no sound came out.

"I see you're wearing your old uniform," Georgie observed. When he'd left, Capt. Ricardo had been wearing a new red jacket made of Iowa pig suede. He wore the jacket at all times, indoors and out, commenting that as he got older, the *Endocrine* seemed to get chillier.

Georgie continued, "Would you like a new uniform, Captain? Should I order the seamstress to stitch up another jacket for you?"

Ricardo nodded, extended two fingers in a command gesture, and croaked, "Make it sew."

Next, Dacron went back to rescue the Pros. They'd taken refuge in a grove of trees as the Civil War raged around them. The Pros practically fell over each other rushing to get into the just-in-time machine—except for Capt. Smirk, who maintained a veneer of casualness.

Smirk ambled into the machine, then gestured back

toward the open field just beyond. "Mr. Dacron," he said, "would you retrieve our Tardy? It's sustained some minor damage."

The Tardy had been smashed by a cannonball; Dacron took along a broom and dustpan as he went to pick it up. Meanwhile, Dr. Flusher opened the first-aid compartment of Dacron's vehicle and found an inflatable pillow for Smirk to sit on.

Dacron carried in the pieces of the Tardy. Then he told the Pros to fasten their seat belts for the ride back.

At first they were all in a jovial mood, grateful just to be safe again; but by the time the just-in-time machine docked in the *Endocrine*'s shuttlebay, several of the Pros had managed to start an argument over who was at fault for their disastrous mission.

Finally Capt. Smirk ordered them to knock it off. They couldn't afford to waste time, he observed, pointing out that the Cons were already hard at work repairing their time machine for another try. As their teammates started reassembling the Tardy, Dr. Flusher took Smirk to Sick Bay to administer a hippospray for his stabbing pains.

Counselor Troit realized that the Pros would do anything to get the jump on the Cons, and vice versa. She sensed this with her remarkable Betavoid telepathy, as well as the fact that they were shouting and waving their fists at each other. On Troit's advice, Dacron locked up his just-in-time machine so neither group could use it.

With everybody back on board, the Neuts were forced to look busy again, so Dacron returned to his console on the Bridge. Within a few minutes his workaholic nature reasserted itself, and he actually was busy. Studying the Preview segments they'd viewed earlier, Dacron noticed a significant element in the Herschel/wrekkie timeline. He asked the two captains to come to the Bridge and review what he'd found.

"Well, what is it, Lieutenant? We've got some serious

repairs to do," said Capt. Smirk. Both he and Capt. Ricardo could hardly hold still, so eager were they to return to work on their time machines and be the first to take off.

Dacron told them, "I have discovered that the moment in which Herschel discovers the videotape is a focal point of the entire time spectrum as we know it."

He pointed to a blip on the Preview screen. "The universe seems to be collapsing toward this event. It is a sort of black hole in time. If one of your groups is able to reach and participate in this moment, thus altering it slightly, the timeline will be repaired. If not, our entire past, present and future will cease to exist. I just thought you would like to know."

Both captains pretended to be professionally concerned about this possibility. Their expressions were somber, but the shifting of their eyes gave them away. They looked like cyclists sizing each other up near the end of a race, jockeying for position, trying to determine who would begin the sprint for the finish line.

Dacron continued, "Since my just-in-time machine has proven the most accurate so far, I could use it to reach Herschel and prevent the destruction of the universe—though the Prime Time Directive prohibits me from interfering further on behalf of either of your groups."

"No, thank you, Lieutenant. We'll manage on our own," said Smirk. He ran his finger over the forward consoles, pretending to inspect them for dust, all the while sidling toward the Crewmover.

Ricardo announced loudly, "Thank you for your report, Mr. Dacron. I believe I'll think it over in my Ready Room." He strode toward the Ready Room door, but at the last second he pivoted and dashed toward the Crewmover. Smirk, crying out in dismay over letting himself be duped, broke into a run.

Ricardo reached the Crewmover first. He jumped in and hit the "door closed" button. Smirk flung himself forward, jamming his torso between the closing doors.

The Crewmover, sensing an obstacle, began to open the doors. "Emergency override!" cried Ricardo, and the doors started closing on Smirk again.

"Belay that order!" yelled Smirk, and the doors slid open. He wedged himself into the Crewmover before Ricardo could stop him. As the doors finally shut tight, the two passengers tried to outshout each other with instructions to the Crewmover: "Deck 15!" "No, Deck 79!" "15!" "79!"

When the Pros and the Cons went to bed that night, they each left a sentry guarding their time machines. And sometime around midnight, each of their sentries decided to take matters into his own hands.

Checkout, who was supposed to be guarding the Pros' machine, crept away from his post and tiptoed toward the Cons' workshop. He wanted to break out of his role as the group wimp by doing something heroic; sabotaging their opponents' machine would fill the bill. Checkout decided the damage should be subtle, so the Cons wouldn't know anything was wrong until after they'd wasted more time in the race.

At the same moment, Wart left his guard post at the Cons' machine and headed for the Pros' workshop. Wart chafed at playing defense; he was better on offense, and he decided it was time to take the battle to the enemy. Besides, he was fed up with the way his fellow Cons always ignored his advice; this was one instance, he decided, where violence would take its rightful place.

The two sentries missed seeing each other as they sneaked through the ship's corridors. In the Cons' workshop, Checkout made some subtle adjustments in the funhouse control panel. Meanwhile, Wart sabotaged the Tardy's time-setting device and, in a stylish parting gesture, planted a time bomb on board.

6

The Days and Nights of Yasha Tar

EARLY THE NEXT morning, the Cons took off in their funhouse. As they approached their designated co-ordinates in the future, everything seemed to be in order.

"We're definitely heading toward Earth this time," said Capt. Ricardo as they sat in the control room watching the observation screen. "Look, there's a movie theater."

Looming ahead was The Centiplex, which advertised "100 Screens / No Waiting." As the Cons' time machine flew past the marquee, they could make out a few titles, including "Terminator #689" and "Three Men and an Old Hag."

The time machine passed through the lobby and landed in one of the 100 screening rooms inside. The Cons stepped out into the darkened theater; it was deserted.

Wart checked the doors. They were locked from the outside. McCaw investigated the fire escapes at the front of the theater; they, too, were locked.

"Even if we're at the right time, this isn't the right place," said Ricardo. "It looks like we'll need help again." He touched his communicator button. "*Endocrine,* this is Capt. Ricardo. Come in." There was no answer.

"Something must be blocking the signal," Smock speculated, "perhaps the construction materials of this building, or something in the surrounding atmosphere."

"What is it with these communicators?" Ricardo grumped. "They always break down when we need them most. Well, since we can't contact the ship for information, let's get out of here and try again. How long will it take, Mr. Snot?"

Snot re-entered the funhouse to find out. After a few moments of tinkering in the control room, he came out and announced, "Someone's fooled wi' the works. Our locator was off by decades, and the homing device is ruined. The machine won't get us out of here."

Just then music began to play, and the movie screen lit up with a message:

> Welcome to the Centiplex Complex. For the viewing enjoyment of those around you, please refrain from smoking, talking, screaming, or changing your infant's diaper in the theater.
>
> And now for our feature presentation.

All the Cons sat down to watch, mesmerized by the wide screen.

The film opened with a shot of two men sitting on a stage. They introduced themselves to the camera.

"Hello, I'm Gene Thickskull, film critic of the *Chicago Tribeaut,*" said one.

"And I'm Roger Eatbert, film critic of the *Chicago Fun Times,*" said the other. "Welcome to the Yasha Tar Film Festival."

"What?" gasped Ricardo.

"What is the matter, Captain?" asked Smock.

Capt. Ricardo replied, "Yasha Tar is one of my former crewmembers. But she died years ago on an away mission. How in the world did her life become a film festival?"

Smock shrugged. "It appears that her timeline had greater significance than you originally thought, Captain," he answered.

Eatbert continued, "We're here to critique the films you're about to see—to throw in our two cents' worth, if you will."

"Or in your case, Roger, one cent's worth," commented Thickskull.

Eatbert shot a dirty glance at Thickskull, then resumed his spiel. "All the films are an offshoot of the 'wrekkie' cult sparked by the discovery of a videotape made by Yasha's crewmate Westerly Flusher. His film generated rabid interest in the crew of the USS *Endocrine*. . . ."

Capt. Ricardo muttered, "That bloody videotape! I'm going to yank it out of the hands of this Herschel character if it's the last thing I do."

". . . and as the wrekkies searched the Starfreak archives," Eatbert continued, "they found more tapes of the *Endocrine* crew—tapes made by anti-shoplifting security cameras that used to film continuously throughout the ship. The wrekkies assembled the footage into individual episodes. On this program we'll focus on the episodes in which Yasha Tar plays a prominent role.

"We'll briefly review the films in the order they were released, pass judgment on them—"

"And most importantly," Thickskull interrupted him, "we'll tell whether or not I could identify with the characters. Let's start with Yasha's debut, 'Encounter at Ballpoint.' "

They showed a brief film clip. Ricardo and Wart stared at it, simultaneously fascinated and repelled to see themselves caught unawares by the camera.

"Well, Gene," Eatbert said when the clip ended, "it wasn't Yasha's finest moment, but with an ensemble cast all having to be introduced at once, that's understandable."

"Yasha had a better chance to show her talents in the second feature, 'The Naked Cow,' " Thickskull said. "I loved the way she explored the final frontier: sex with a machine. Talk about boldly going where no one has gone before!"

"Calm down, Gene," Eatbert urged. "Keep your sweater

"On this program we'll focus on the episodes in which Yasha Tar plays a prominent role."

tucked in. Yasha's next biggie was 'Commode of Honor.' Unfortunately we don't have any footage from that episode, because on the night it was broadcast we misprogrammed our VCR and taped 'Wheel of Fortune' by mistake."

Next the critics presented a scene from "Skin of Exxon" showing Yasha getting knocked off by a mean-tempered oil slick.

Starting to rise from his theater seat, Smock asked, "I suppose that's the end of the storyline, Captain?"

"No, Mr. Smock. Not by a long shot," Ricardo said. Smock sat back down.

Eatbert announced, "Now the fun really begins. In 'Time Lag-acy,' Yasha Tar's sister, Fresh Tar, turns up as a terrorist on the late Yasha's home world."

Wart spoke up. "I am tired of hearing them *talk* about the films," he groused. "I want to *see* the films, and not just tiny clips, either!" The others caught his cranky mood.

"Yeah, show the movies already!" McCaw hollered at the screen.

"Get on wi' it!" shouted Snot. "We want movies!"

Ricardo, trying to act like one of the guys for a change, but utterly unfamiliar with rowdiness, managed only: "Make it show!"

Next, the film played scenes from "Yesterday's *Endocrine*," in which the *Endocrine C-Sick* accidentally traveled ahead of its timeline, bringing Yasha Tar into the future. Only Guano, through some mysterious process, knew that Yasha did not belong in the present because she had been cancelled two seasons before. The film clip showed Ricardo sending Yasha back to her death in the *Endocrine C-Sick*.

"Captain, how could you?" murmured Smock.

"She requested the transfer herself," Ricardo countered. "Besides, that's still not the end of the story. Keep watching."

Sure enough, the next clip, from "Beyond Redemption," revealed that Yasha had not died in the *Endocrine C-Sick* after all. She was taken prisoner by a Romanumen commander; he married her and fathered a daughter who looked remarkably like Yasha except for an updated hairdo and some snazzy eyebrows.

The daughter grew up to be a Romanumen commander like her father. She tried to split the Federation by backing a conspiracy among the Kringles, led by Duras-Cell. But even though the Romanumens lent the conspirators their technologically advanced ships, fully equipped with croaking devices, ultimately the takeover failed.

"Say, that woman looked familiar," Smock remarked. The clip ended, and Thickskull and Eatbert came back onscreen.

"And we haven't heard the last of Yasha's Romanumen daughter," Eatbert observed. "She popped up again in 'Eunuchation,' a rare two-episode story featuring the return of the famous Mr. Smock."

Thickskull chimed in, "Part one made *The Guinness Book of World Records* for the shortest onscreen appearance of a heavily hyped guest star. As a matter of fact, Smock had a bigger part in the 'Coming Attractions' trailer than he did in the actual episode." The critics sat back to watch scenes from the two programs.

"Now I remember," Smock said. "She foiled my secret peace mission that attempted to reunite the Vultures and the Romanumens." The onscreen action showed the conclusion, in which the *Endocrine* crew overcame the evildoers and Yasha's daughter slunk off stage left, muttering, "Curses, foiled again."

"*That's* the end," Ricardo announced. "As far as I know, anyway."

The screen went black for a moment. Then it lit up with a shot of two men sitting on a stage. It was Thickskull and Eatbert again. They introduced themselves to the camera.

"Hello, I'm Gene Thickskull, film critic of the *Chicago Tribeaut.*"

"And I'm Roger Eatbert, film critic of the *Chicago Fun Times.* Welcome to the Yasha Tar Film Festival."

"Hey, this is the same as before," Wart protested.

"We're here to critique the films you're about to see . . ." Eatbert said.

"It's started over!" Snot shouted. "We're stuck in a time loop! Help! Help!"

Snot and McCaw panicked and scrambled for the exit. They got into a fistfight over who would pass through the door first, oblivious to the fact that it was locked anyway. Wart, enraged over the prospect of being stuck in a time loop, began uprooting the theater seats and throwing them at the screen.

"Captain, may I remind you," said Smock, "that the longer we remain trapped here, the greater the likelihood that the Pros will reach Herschel first."

"Oh dear, oh dear," fretted Capt. Ricardo, fingering his worry beads.

7

The City on the Edge of Foreclosure

"I DON'T BELIEVE this. I just don't believe it. Why me?!" Capt. Smirk raised his arms to the heavens as if he were soliciting an answer, and Piker stared at the ground in embarrassment. The others followed them out of the Tardy and looked around.

"Does this look like the Maplewood, New Jersey of the future to you, Commander? Does it?" Smirk demanded.

Piker's face reddened. "No, sir."

"No, it isn't," Smirk went on. "Let me tell you where—and when—we've come to, because my crew has been here before."

They stood in a barren landscape amidst scattered rocks. Before them stood an imposing arch made of stone. The arch flashed as it spoke to them: "I am the Guardian of Reruns. Step through me and view the past."

Smirk continued to harangue Piker. "Last time we were here, we stepped through that arch, straight into the Earth of the 1930s. But I really had no great desire to visit there again."

Smirk paused, caught his breath, and opened his mouth to resume his tirade; then he stopped himself. Even though Piker had obviously misprogrammed their time machine again, it was futile to correct his thought processes when he probably didn't even have any.

"Captain," Checkout called. He was examining the Tardy's control box. Smirk joined him.

"Someone has tampered vith the time-control mechanism," Checkout observed, pointing to the panel, which was smashed into dozens of pieces.

"Hmmmph," said Smirk, realizing that perhaps this time their inaccurate landing was not Piker's fault after all. As he turned toward Piker to apologize, he saw Piker stepping through the arch.

"Commander, no!" Smirk shouted, but Piker had already gone to the other side.

"We've got to follow him. Everyone must stay together!" said Smirk, herding the others toward the arch. "Let's go. Hurry!"

"Captain, I'm frightened," Yoohoo whinnied.

Passing through the arch, they found themselves on a street corner of an American city in the early 1930s. Piker was already there, looking around. "Sir," he said to Smirk, "I thought this arch might give us an alternate means of time travel."

"Well, it won't," Smirk snapped. "It's not going to get us to the future, anyway. Now don't touch anything. We've all got to leave at the same time. Let's get out of here before we affect this timeline."

Piker wasn't listening. He watched anxiously as a woman stepped off the curb, oblivious to the fire engine which was bearing down on her, bells clanging and siren wailing. "Look out!" Piker yelled, grabbing the woman and pushing her back to safety on the curb. Unfortunately he forgot to remove himself from harm's way, and the side mirror of the fire engine clipped his head.

"Thank you, sir," the woman chirped as she walked away. Piker rubbed his head, his expression more vacant than usual.

Smirk rushed up to Piker. "Now you've really done it!" Smirk scolded him. "You never should have saved that woman's life."

Piker gazed at him groggily. "Sir?"

"That woman," Smirk continued, "is Edith Keebler. The last time my crew was here, Dr. McCaw made the same mistake: he saved her life. Though that seems like the right thing to do, it isn't.

"You see, she's a social worker with two possible futures. In one, she dies. That's the timeline you just screwed up. In the other—her alternate future—she lives, becoming a leading pacifist in the Keebler Elves Peace and Cookie Movement. She's instrumental in delaying America's entry into World War II until it's too late and the Nazis have already developed superior chocolate chips. Do you understand, Commander?"

Piker nodded. He didn't understand, but he'd learned in Starfreak Academy that as long as he didn't admit it, the teachers would leave him alone.

"So for history to come out correctly, Edith Keebler must die now," Smirk concluded. "And since you just prevented her accidental death, we're going to have to kill her ourselves."

"Yes, sir." Piker pulled out his phaser and switched it from its usual "Stun" setting to the "Terminate with Extreme Prejudice" setting. Smirk grabbed his arm.

"No, Commander, not the phaser," said Smirk. "It's too dangerous to introduce advanced technology into the past."

Piker scratched his head. "You mean like when Capt. Ricardo talks about how we have to keep the timeline intact, as our solemn duty to posterity?"

"No, I mean that it's my solemn duty not to get stuck here in the 1930s," said Smirk. "Remember how the Confederates got hold of one of our phasers and almost vaporized us? It would be tragic if I couldn't resume my place among the classy dames of the future." *I shouldn't have to remind him of this—especially about all the women who are counting on me,* Smirk thought. *Mr. Smock would have known that implicitly. Maybe I won't offer*

Piker a position on my crew after all. Smirk continued, "You're going to have to kill Edith in some way that's appropriate to this era."

"I see." Piker put the phaser away and looked down the street. Edith Keebler, who'd been walking away from them, was about halfway down the block. Piker jumped into a taxi at curbside. "Follow that woman!" he directed.

"The one in the red sedan?" the taxi driver responded.

"No, the one on the sidewalk in the brown coat."

The driver stared at him. "Why don't you follow her yourself, buddy? Just get out and walk!"

"You don't understand," Piker urged him. "I want you to run her over."

Piker sprawled at Smirk's feet after the driver had kicked him out of the cab and sped away. As Piker picked himself up and prepared to follow Edith Keebler on foot, Smirk stopped him.

"Wait, Commander," said Smirk. "Don't kill her just yet. I think I've fallen in love with her."

Piker was puzzled. "She's not really your type, is she, sir? She hasn't got a beehive hairdo, she's not wearing chiffon . . ."

"But look at all that heavy eye makeup," crooned Smirk as he gazed at Keebler, who was crossing the street against the light. "She's got that anachronistic charm that makes me shiver." A car swerved to avoid Keebler and struck a lamppost head-on; she kept walking heedlessly. "Look, Commander, I know we can't let her survive indefinitely, but just let me be with her a little while, maybe spend the evening courting her. In the morning we'll talk about what to do."

Piker nodded. "You're the boss," he said.

The five Pros followed Keebler to her workplace, a cookie kitchen that gave free handouts to the poor. As they reached the head of the line and loaded their supper plates with Elfkin Bite-Size Sandwich Cookies, Smirk felt the stab of his recurring shoulder pain. Edith Keebler, doling out cookies, noticed him wince and came around the counter to help him.

"Are you all right?" Keebler asked, touching Smirk's shoulder.

"It's nothing," Smirk said with a grimace. "Just an old football injury."

"Really? You're a football player?" Keebler began massaging his shoulder, and Smirk gave her a syrupy smile.

"Quarterback," said Smirk. "Ummm, that feels good." He flexed the shoulder she was rubbing.

"I'm trained in therapeutic massage techniques," Keebler told him. "Are any other parts of your body giving you trouble?"

"Not at the moment, but I'm sure I could come up with something by this evening," Smirk responded. "Could I walk you home?"

"Well, I'm the only worker on duty here, and there are so many hungry people to be fed"—Keebler looked at the line, which filled the room and stretched out the door—"and if I don't stay on the job they'll all go to bed hungry tonight... oh, what the heck. Sure, you can walk me home. Let's go."

Keebler grabbed her coat. They passed the cookie line and went out the door, with Smirk giving Piker a thumbs-up gesture behind Keebler's back.

As the two walked through the city streets, getting to know each other, Smirk was impressed by Keebler's inborn talent for remaining unscathed and unaware while causing mayhem all around her. Five blocks and six major traffic accidents later, Smirk knew he loved Edith Keebler.

It wasn't her mind that attracted him; he mistrusted pacifists, since they always seemed intent on making the universe unnecessarily boring. No, he loved her exotic beauty and her glamorous makeup, so totally unlikely in a social worker living in Depression-era America.

Yes, this was love, all right. They even had music playing in the background. It came from a radio sitting in a storefront; the song was "Goodnight, Sweetheart."

Where have I heard that recently? Smirk wondered. *Ah, yes. Dacron was singing it in the shower at the gym.* Dacron's falsetto had startled Smirk, who thought for a moment that there was a woman in the locker room.

Smirk deliberately brought his thoughts back to the present. Keebler was ushering him into her apartment. This would be a night of exquisite poignancy, Smirk knew: wooing a total stranger with the knowledge that the next day she would be totally out of the picture, stone-cold dead. This was romance just the way he liked it.

Smirk's peace of mind lasted only until the next morning, when he and Piker had a philosophical discussion about which one of them should kill Edith Keebler.

"You do it."

"I don't want to do it. You do it."

"I don't wanna do it either. You do it."

"No, you do it."

Piker had been having second thoughts about the whole thing. His most serious worry was that killing Keebler would affect the cookie timeline. Perhaps when they returned to the 24th century, there would be no more Pecan Sandies.

Finally Smirk gave Piker a direct order to knock off Keebler. Piker couldn't use his phaser, and it took him till midafternoon to come up with an alternate weapon. Then he spent several more hours lugging it up to the rooftop of a five-story building.

Finally, everything was ready. The safe which Piker had borrowed from a nearby merchant hung precariously from a rope off the rooftop. Piker scanned the passersby until he spotted Edith Keebler. He waited as she approached his drop site; then he released the rope. The safe plunged toward the sidewalk.

The safe plunged toward the sidewalk.

That evening, as they waited their turn in the cookie line where Edith Keebler was handing out Pitter Patter Peanut Butter Cremes, Smirk muttered to Piker, "She's still here. What happened?"

"I tried dropping a safe on her, but she swerved at the last second and accidentally knocked someone else into the spot I was aiming for," said Piker.

"A safe?" Smirk rolled his eyes. "Was the other person killed?"

Piker nodded. "Instantly."

"It wasn't anybody crucial to World War II, was it? Remember, we have to keep this timeline intact. Everything has to happen the way it was meant to."

"No, nobody special," Piker answered, wishing he'd paid more attention in history class so he'd know for sure whether or not this George S. Patton guy was really important.

The next morning, Piker lurked in the alley waiting for Keebler to pass by on her way to work. He'd hidden a bundle of dynamite under a pile of rags on the sidewalk; its long fuse extended to his hiding place. Any minute now, as Keebler approached, he'd light the fuse.

He spotted Keebler and watched as she crossed in the middle of the street, causing a busload of orphans to swerve out of her way and go into a tailspin. As she headed toward the pile of rags, Piker lit his match.

Smirk glared at Piker over his breakfast tray of Chips Deluxe. "Well?" he demanded, indicating with a jerk of his head that Keebler was still very much among the living.

"How did I know that Salvation Army band was going to get in the way?" Piker protested. "I can't believe she came through it without a scratch. The dynamite even drove a trombone through a mailbox. You should have seen it."

"Never mind," Smirk said. "Just do this and get it over

with, will you? Try to get her on her way home tonight."

That does it, Smirk thought. *Piker has screwed up one time too many. I'm taking him off my payroll. Wait a minute, I never put him on my payroll. Well, I'm definitely keeping him off the payroll, then.*

Piker slumped against a lamppost, watching the door of the cookie kitchen, wondering how he was going to make another attempt on Keebler's life when he had neither a plan nor a weapon. *I don't think I'll try for a job on Captain Smirk's crew after all,* he thought. *Not only does he constantly demand that I think, I don't even get time-and-a-half pay for it.*

He was so preoccupied with his predicament that he missed seeing Keebler come out the door. By the time he realized she was leaving, she was halfway down the street, about to disappear into the crowd.

Piker strode after her, dodging pedestrians left and right. "Excuse me, excuse me," he said.

He had almost caught up, but a mother pushing a baby buggy still blocked his path. Piker accidentally clipped the mother, knocking the buggy against Keebler's leg.

Keebler lost her balance, hovered on the curb for a moment with arms flailing, then fell into the street directly in the path of a steamroller. The steamroller lumbered over Keebler and continued on its way.

Piker stared in fascination at the mosaic of Keebler's body; it had retained its shape, if not its thickness, and now covered about a quarter of the city block. He realized Capt. Smirk had caught up to them and was also staring at Keebler's remains.

"Gee," Piker observed, "she looks a lot like Wile E. Coyote in the 'Road Runner Road Repairs' cartoon that was on last Saturday."

The five Pros leapt out of the Guardian of Reruns arch and stood in the barren field near their Tardy.

The arch spoke. "The timeline has returned to normal. All is as it was before, except for the gray hair of Communications Officer Yoohoo, which could definitely use some Grecian Formula."

At that moment Wart's time bomb exploded, sending pieces of the Tardy flying everywhere. None of the Pros were hurt, but the prospect of being stranded again, and letting the Cons get to Herschel first, left them sitting around in stunned silence.

"You people aren't having the best of luck, are you?" the Guardian observed archly.

8

Rescue Redux

MEANWHILE, BACK ON the *Endocrine,* the Neuts were involved in their latest scientific project: a scavenger hunt.

Dacron had dreamed up the scavenger hunt to relieve the Neuts' boredom. He'd given Zulu permission to disassemble him and hide his body parts throughout the ship. Only Dacron's left hand remained on the Bridge, resting on the arm of the Captain's chair, just in case an emergency came up. The hand could work the Captain's control buttons and even had hearing capabilities, thanks to a microchip in its pinky.

Prowling around the ship on level 64½, Guano spotted a scavenger item half-hidden behind a thermostat. She ran up and grabbed it; it was one of Dacron's ears.

Guano checked the score sheet. "Only ten points!" she complained to herself. "Hardly worth carrying back to the Bridge!" Nevertheless, she stashed the ear in her enormous hat, along with her cosmetics case, credit cards, a picnic lunch, and the unabridged second edition of *Webster's New Twentieth Century Dictionary.*

"Dis is Lt. Checkout to *Endocrine. Endocrine,* do you read me?" Checkout whispered urgently into his communicator insignia.

Despite his high hopes, Checkout hadn't gained any

status by telling his fellow Pros that the Cons were probably stranded, too, since he'd sabotaged their time machine. "Anybody can *wreck* a machine," Yoohoo had responded. "If you're so smart, why can't you fix our machine instead, and get us out of here?" Then they'd all lapsed back into their funk.

So now Checkout was crouched behind some rocks about ten yards away from the others, hoping to summon some help. He had to keep his voice down so Capt. Smirk wouldn't discover him trying to call the ship. Smirk had insisted that somehow they would get themselves out of this fix. Checkout was sure they couldn't; he hoped Dacron would rescue them again with his just-in-time machine.

"*Endocrine,* come in, please," whispered Checkout. He held the communicator to his ear and turned the volume up a notch.

His hopes rose when he heard a signal coming through. But instead of the voice of an *Endocrine* crewmember, he heard music playing. Checkout listened for awhile, then realized it was the theme music from the daytime drama "Daze of Our Lives."

"*Endocrine,* come in, please. Mayday. Mayday," Checkout hissed as loudly as he dared.

The music stopped. Checkout continued, "*Endocrine,* dis is Checkout. Ve are stranded here next to da Guardian of Reruns. Can you get a lock on our position? Can you rescue us?"

A series of taps came through the communicator. Checkout realized he was hearing a message in Morse Code. His translation skills were rusty, but he pulled out a pencil and paper anyway and frantically jotted down his interpretation as the message came through:

'Twas Brillo, and the slimy gloves
Did perspire and gamble in the babe

Reading over what he'd written, Checkout decided to get help. He crept back toward the group and caught Yoohoo's eye. He motioned for her to join him and held a finger to his mouth to indicate she should keep quiet about it. Yoohoo stood up, stretching and yawning elaborately, and pretended she was simply taking a walk as she made her way to Checkout's hiding place.

"What is it?" she asked. He led her out of earshot of the group.

"I've contacted da ship," he told her, "and asked for rescue, but I don't understand deir answer. Tell me vat you tink." He handed her his insignia device.

Instantly recognizing the Morse Code, Yoohoo transformed into her briskly efficient communicator's posture, pressing the receiver to one ear while sticking a finger in her other ear to block out distractions. "Say again, *Endocrine,*" Yoohoo requested.

Checkout handed her the pencil and paper, and she translated the code:

> *Message received stop will rescue you as soon as I get myself together stop love Dacron*

• • •

"Has Zulu found my arms yet, Counselor?" Dacron asked. He stood on the Bridge, reassembled except for his upper limbs.

"Not exactly, Dacron," Troit told him, "but at least we're getting closer. Remember how Zulu thought he'd hidden them in a cupboard? Well, Georgie realized Zulu had accidentally thrown them down a laundry chute. Georgie and Zulu are down in the laundry room now, looking for them."

"Ah," said Dacron. "Then I will begin the rescue attempt armlessly."

"Can't you use your hand?" asked Troit, glancing at Dacron's left hand, which was still lying on the Captain's chair.

"No," said Dacron. "The battery needs recharging. Apparently my hand did a lot of work while I was away. But do not be concerned, Counselor. I can prepare the just-in-time machine without the use of my arms." He entered the machine, which the others had carried onto the Bridge for him, and began pressing its control buttons with his nose.

Meanwhile, at the Bridge's Tactical station, Guano tried to decipher the communication panel so they could contact Capt. Ricardo and the Cons. No messages had come from them in a while, and the Neuts were concerned that they too were stranded again.

"This thing isn't very user-friendly," Guano grumbled, staring at the panel.

"It's probably still in DOS," Troit suggested. "Why don't you call up the Idiotspeak program? Just type in DORK, then press Enter."

Guano did. "Hey, that's better," she said brightly. "The communicator says our signal to the Cons is being blocked, apparently by a large concentration of industrial-sized popcorn machines. But it does give us coordinates so we can find the Cons and pick them up."

Georgie and Zulu emerged from the Crewmover onto the Bridge. "Where's Dacron?" Georgie asked. "We found his arms." Hearing this, Dacron stepped out of the just-in-time machine.

"Hey, Dacron," said Georgie in a tone of forced cheerfulness. "Got the ol' arms for you." He held them out.

Dacron looked a little taken aback. "They seem to be several sizes smaller than when they were removed," Dacron observed.

"Uh, yeah, they might be," admitted Georgie. "They were already in the dryer when we found them, and I guess they've shrunk." He clicked them into Dacron's arm sockets. The wrists dangled at the level of Dacron's ribcage.

"I'm terribly sorry about this, Commander," said Zulu.

"Fortunately, I am not able to bear a grudge," Dacron

The wrists dangled at the level of Dacron's ribcage.

told him. "However, if and when I ever acquire emotion, I may look back on this incident with a slightly different viewpoint."

Georgie snapped Dacron's hands into place. "Well, we can try stretching your arms," Georgie offered. Dacron agreed to try it, so Zulu and Georgie each took an arm and began to pull.

With all his parts intact and stretched back into shape, Dacron had little trouble piloting his time machine to rescue the Pros and Cons again.

But Dacron's hopes that everyone would finally begin to cooperate in their efforts to reach Herschel were soon dashed. Both captains were as eager as ever to perfect their own time machines and beat the other to the punch.

Dacron reminded them that the entire known universe would be wiped out if somebody didn't reach Herschel soon. But Smirk merely told him that the Pros were bound to hit the mark on their next try, and Ricardo said the same thing about the Cons.

Dacron doubted it. He figured that unless their time machines were adjusted to a goof-proof level, they had little chance of getting to Herschel. Somebody had to do the tune-up, and Dacron decided he was just the android for the job.

To lure the Pros' and Cons' sentries away from their overnight security watch on the time machines, Dacron set off a hull-breach drill.

When the alarm sounded for the drill, the sentries, like everyone else, left their posts to practice the procedure they would follow in the event of an actual hull breach: crouch in the southeast corner of the room beneath heavy furniture and prepare to explode.

While the sentries were gone, Dacron sneaked into the time machines. He found their control panels incredibly primitive. The best he could do was to rig each of them with a guidance device, so that even if they landed at the wrong point again, they'd eventually be drawn to Herschel. It was up to the Pros and Cons not to screw up in any other unforeseen, creative way; Dacron hoped that at least one of the groups could manage that.

9

Childhood's Dead End

"IT'S A 'SEVEN.' "

"No, it's a 'one.' "

"How can it be a 'one'? Look at that big hook at the top. That makes it a 'seven' for sure."

"No. If it were a 'seven' I would have drawn a line through the lower part, like this." Beverage grabbed the pen from Piker and dashed a stroke through the numeral. "That's the way it's taught in Penmanship."

"Oh, right. Flaunt your postgraduate education at us again," Piker retorted.

"Will you two stop it?" Smirk snarled, and they broke off, pouting. "Who cares what number Beverage wrote down? Obviously, Cmdr. Piker misinterpreted it, for whatever reason, and misdialed again. Now where the heck are we?"

The Tardy had landed inside a room. It looked ordinary, yet there was something forbidding about it. The Pros peered through the Tardy's glass walls, afraid to step out.

"I've seen dis somevhere before," Checkout mused. "In a movie or sometink. Maybe it vas a trainink film."

Yoohoo, facing the rear of the booth, gasped, "Look!"

The others turned as quickly as they could, considering that they were jammed into the Tardy like canned sardines. From out of nowhere, the image of a fetus had appeared, hovering in midair beyond the Tardy.

In an instant that image was replaced by one of an old man sitting at a table. He turned toward them, observed them placidly for a moment, then resumed eating his fourteen-inch pizza with cheese and mushrooms which nestled in a paper wrapper that proclaimed it "The BEST Pizza in TOWN!"

"Vy, dat's Dave," Checkout gasped.

"Dave who?" Beverage asked.

"Vatch," Checkout said, pointing at the man. "Next ve'll see him on his deathbed."

"Eeeeuuuww," squealed Yoohoo squeamishly.

Sure enough, the next image showed the old man in bed, with only an intravenous line of Jolt Cola keeping him alive.

"What's going on?" Piker demanded.

"It's some kind of flashback showink his lifetime," Checkout said. "Dat fetus was him, and so vas the man vith the pizza, and dis old man, too."

"Yeah, right," Piker scoffed.

"Why are we being shown his lifetime? We don't even know him," Beverage said.

"But there's somebody we do know." Smirk pointed to the side. "That's Smock's parents."

A new image had appeared, showing Smock's Vulture father assisting his human wife Amandate in the labor room. The Pros realized they were witnessing Smock's birth.

A nurse bundled the newborn Smock in a blanket and handed him to the Vulture. "Congratulations, Ambassador Shark," she said. "You have a son."

Smock's father stared impassively at the newborn, then grunted. "Hmmph," he said. "His features are decidedly human. I do not approve. Please put him back."

The image disappeared as mysteriously as it had come. "Checkout, what is this?" Smirk asked.

"It's difficult to explain, Keptin," Checkout said. "Ve have landed in a room vich displays significant events

"It's some kind of flashback showink his lifetime,"
Checkout said.

Smock's father stared impassively at the newborn.

someone vants us to see. And since it began vay back vith Mr. Smock's birth, I believe ve are in for a massive rerun."

Everybody groaned.

Checkout was right. Outside the Tardy, a series of images unfolded before the Pros' eyes. Each segment showed an important episode in the life of one *Endocrine* crewmember:

A teenaged Capt. Smirk beamed as he passed around an article from his high school paper announcing that his class had voted him "Most Likely to Father an Alien Child."

Dr. McCaw, as a young medical student, moonlighted as a cadaver in Anatomy Lab to help earn his way through medical school.

Checkout, on his sixth try for his pilot's license, backed into the instructor's shuttle while maneuvering out of the shuttlebay.

Yoohoo, at her previous job before joining Smirk's crew, chirped, "Thank you for using AT&T."

Mr. Snot, in one of his pre-*Endocrine* jobs, wore coveralls with "Ajax Heating & Cooling" stitched on the front pocket. Standing in front of a disassembled furnace, he told a distraught homeowner, "I've never seen th' likes of it. It'll have to go into th' shop."

Guano donned her first of many enormous hats, hiding the fact that her brain had quadrupled in size since she'd taken the Evelyn Woodpecker speed-reading course.

Capt. Ricardo was elected the first president of a newly-formed union that would later become Starfreak: the Hairline Pilots' Association.

Piker, as an infant, was accidentally dropped on his head from atop a 50-foot Alaskan glacier.

Deanna Troit, on her second birthday, opened her gifts: a doll, a harmonica, and a training bra.

Dacron was undergoing assembly by Dr. Nubian Spittoon. Nearby in the laboratory stood some earlier android prototypes: Dacron's brother Lycra and his sisters Polly Esther, Silke, and Lynnen.

Guano donned her first of many enormous hats.

Wart retrofitted a toy rifle into a working weapon and stormed the principal's office to dramatize the demand of his kindergarten class for chocolate milk at snack time.

Georgie created his visor in a high school shop class by welding a muffler grill onto his girlfriend's hairband.

Beverage, planning her wedding to Jock Crusher, registered her Tupperware pattern at Sears.

The series of images ended. "Now what?" Smirk asked.

"If it goes like I tink it vill," said Checkout, "ve'll now see lots of colors and veird psychedelic effects. Ve'll also be squished into two dimensions."

"Will it hurt?" whimpered Yoohoo.

"Only if you're overveight," Checkout said. Yoohoo began to wail.

Piker checked the Tardy's readout. "Captain, we're sliding forward in time toward our target date. Somehow it's become locked into the Tardy's automatic time-finder. We could be the ones to reach Herschel after all."

"But first we've got to survive this two-dimensional business," Smirk said as the Tardy began slipping toward a kaleidoscopic horizon. "Hang on, everybody!"

10

That Was Then . . . This Is Nuts

"I DON'T UNDERSTAND what's so hard about controlling something as elementary as this time machine!" Capt. Ricardo raged.

"I know ye don't understand, mon! That's why I have t' do th' dirrrty work for ye!" Snot yelled back.

The two of them stood arguing nose-to-nose outside Snot's funhouse. On their third try, the Cons had landed on the Bridge of the *Endocrine*—20 years in the future.

"Gentlemen," Smock interrupted, "rather than arguing over who is to blame for this miscalculation, it would be more productive to explore our surroundings. This is a priceless opportunity to glimpse the near future—"

"Make it so, then, Mr. Smock," Ricardo snapped.

"Sir?" responded Smock.

"Do it," Ricardo explained. "Check out the ship. Give me a full report on what everybody's up to." They hadn't yet glimpsed the crew of 20 years hence; the future-Bridge was deserted, and the ship was on Autopilot.

"Yes, Captain," Smock replied.

Smock's explorations were cut short less than an hour later when Ricardo summoned him over the intercom: "Mr. Smock, report to the time machine immediately."

When Smock arrived, the funhouse was humming

loudly, and the other Cons had already boarded it. Smock joined them in the control room.

"What is happening, Captain?" Smock asked.

"We're not sure," Ricardo answered, "but somehow the time machine started itself. Snot found there's some sort of automatic guidance mechanism at work, and it's set for the target date we've been trying to reach. I believe we'll make it this time."

A moment later the funhouse took off. The Cons watched the monitor as a swirl of events passed before them, interspersed with occasional flying houses, tumbleweeds, and the Wicked Witch of the West.

Snot calculated that the journey would take at least an hour, so they sat on the floor and tried to get comfortable.

"Well, Mr. Smock, this would be a good time to hear what you observed on board the ship 20 years from now," Ricardo said.

"I did manage to find a few crewmembers," Smock reported. "Cmdr. Piker, for instance. He is still receiving a constant stream of job offers for the captaincy of other ships."

"Job offers?" Ricardo echoed. "Why would they want him? How would they hear of him in the first place?"

"I have no idea, Captain," Smock said blandly. "At any rate, he sat at a desk reviewing a tall stack of letters—invitations to assume command of various other Starfreak vessels. He was marking the letters with a rubber stamp that read 'Position Refused / Thanks for Your Interest / Wilson Piker.'

"I also talked to Lt. Cmdr. Dacron. He told me that within the past 20 years he had experienced every possible emotion, but no one was willing to acknowledge it. Also, his body had been inhabited by numerous life forms, such as a grandfatherly scientist, several species of alien beings, and the Avon Lady.

"I caught a glimpse of Guano. She finally got her eyebrow transplant. Unfortunately, the blond shade she chose looks rather artificial.

"The HolidayDeck had expanded to 50 units operating 24 hours a day. They were being administered by a HolidayDeck afficionado named Lt. Retch Barcode.

"There was also an extremely arrogant alien known as Q-Tip."

Ricardo looked surprised. "Q-Tip was on board?"

"He was just visiting," Smock said. "He's now retired, living at the James T. Smirk Home for Incurable Hams. He dared me to justify the existence of the human race. When that taunt failed to arouse me, he challenged my intellect with a series of trivia questions, such as 'What are the names of the seven dwarfs?' "

"Q-Tip," Ricardo mused. "You know, I almost miss him."

"He mentioned you," Smock said. "His exact words were: 'Ask the inimitable captain that if humanity is so advanced, how come his crew still wears uniforms, as if they were all working at McDonald's?' "

"On second thought, I don't really miss him that much," Ricardo added.

"Captain," Snot broke in, pointing to the time indicator, "we're still on target for the moment Herschel finds the videotape. There's no doubt o' it—we'll be the first ones to arrive after all."

None of the Cons could actually bring himself to smile at this good news, but they all looked decidedly less crabby.

Back on the *Endocrine,* Dacron rechecked his console a final time. The readout confirmed his fear: they were in big trouble.

"Attention, fellow crewmembers," said Dacron, paging the Neuts via the intercom. "An extremely urgent situation has developed. I regret to inform you that we must all gather on the Bridge and actually do some work."

After the other Neuts assembled, lounging on the carpet

in the forward section of the Bridge, Dacron set up a podium in front of them and began reading from a sheaf of notes. "Welcome to my 'State of the *Endocrine*' address," he began. "These are historic times for our crew."

Georgie jabbed Zulu with his elbow and whispered, "I think Dacron is letting this temporary-command thing go to his head." Meanwhile, Guano, sensing a long speech in the making, yawned widely while making an elaborate show of consulting her wristwatch.

Dacron continued, "The actions we take in the next few hours could determine whether we live to explore new galaxies or disappear into obscurity like the Samkonian fruit fly with its lifespan of approximately 10.8 nanoseconds.

"Before the Pros and Cons began their latest journey, I installed guidance devices on their time machines. While tracking their progress, I have concluded that the devices are operating perfectly. Too perfectly, in fact. Please, hold your applause." Dacron looked up from his notes; then, since there was no applause, he went on.

"By landing on their target moment in Herschel's home at precisely the same instant, the Pros and Cons will open a time rift, throwing them years further into the future. Such an event will irreversibly alter the space/time continuum. We will be unable to retrieve them, even with my just-in-time machine. In effect, they will have vanished forever."

Dacron paused for a sip from the water glass on his podium, and Guano broke in. "Are you finished? Can we go back to the HolidayDeck now?"

Dacron shook his head. "I need you to take up positions here on the Bridge. We will contact each of the groups and try to persuade them to alter their course slightly, thus preventing this time rift."

Zulu went to the Tactical station's communication console. Dacron and Deanna sat in their command chairs, Georgie took the pilot's seat, and Guano pulled a mixer out of her hat and began to whip up a batch of chocolate milkshakes.

"Mr. Zulu, hail the Pros," Dacron ordered.

" 'Hey, you' frequency open," Zulu responded, "but we've only got an audio signal from them, Commander."

"Attention, Pros. This is Lt. Cmdr. Dacron. Do you read me?"

Capt. Smirk's voice sounded strained. "What is it, Dacron?"

"You are headed for the precise instant when Herschel finds the videotape," Dacron said. "The Cons are about to arrive there also. There is a guidance device in your control mechanism. You must adjust it to offset your arrival by a few seconds, thus preventing a time rift that will throw you ten years into the future and alter the space/time continuum irreversibly."

"I'd like to oblige," came Smirk's reply, "but we're two-dimensional right now, so it would be a little tricky to move the controls. At the moment, my entire body is one molecule thick, and I'm sort of plastered to my chair."

"Oh," said Dacron.

"But thanks for the information," Smirk concluded flatly. "Smirk out."

"Mr. Zulu, hail the Cons," Dacron ordered.

"Cons' time machine answering our hail," reported Zulu. The image of the Cons' control room appeared on the Viewscreen of the Bridge.

"What is it, Dacron?" said Capt. Ricardo from the Viewscreen.

"Sir, your Cons and Captain Smirk's Pros are about to arrive at Herschel's home at the same instant," said Dacron. "This will create a dangerous rift that could leave both of your groups stranded in the future. The Pros are unable to control their course. I suggest that you offset your arrival by several seconds, thus preventing a collision."

"What? And let them beat us to the punch? Balderdash!" Ricardo answered.

"You could arrive *before* them, sir," Dacron suggested.

Ricardo conferred briefly with Smock and Snot, then shook his head. "That is unacceptable," he said. "We'd risk being sucked into the previous time rift that occurred when Cmdr. Piker's videotape arrived at Herschel's home. No, Lieutenant, we'll take our chances on this course." The Cons closed their "hey, you" frequency.

"Well, so much for team spirit," Zulu remarked. He checked his console, then announced, "The collision of the Pros and Cons will occur in ten minutes."

"I believe we should set our course to arrive then also," Dacron stated. "We can accompany them through the time rift to the distant future. It should be an educational experience." The others gave their approval, so Dacron connected the ship's navigation console to the control panel of his just-in-time machine with a three-pronged extension cord.

"Dacron, what are our chances of surviving this rift?" Georgie asked.

"Precisely one in 1,000,000,000," Dacron replied as he set the last of the time controls.

"What?!" screamed Guano. "You want to risk our necks just so you can expand your horizons? Forget it!" She shook her head defiantly, causing the milkshake mixer to teeter dangerously close to the edge of her hat.

"I am afraid it is too late," Dacron replied. "The navigational sequence cannot be discontinued once underway."

Disgusted, Zulu banged his fist on the Tactical station. "Of all the . . . the . . . " he sputtered, " . . . putting us in danger just to satisfy your scientific curiosity . . . "

"Besides," Dacron continued calmly, "I will offset our arrival by a fraction of a second, and we can pause just long enough to alter Herschel's pivotal moment in the space/time continuum. This will halt a black-hole effect that I have detected at those coordinates, which would otherwise obliterate the universe. The Pros and Cons will remain there too briefly to take this action, so we must.

It is, in fact, our only chance for survival."

"Oh," said Guano and Zulu, their frenzy dribbling away like air escaping from a faulty party balloon. Frowning, Guano asked, "Why didn't you tell us that in the first place?"

"I wanted to trigger your typical human overreaction," Dacron replied. "I find it intriguing."

"So we've got one chance in a billion of surviving this experience?" Georgie asked. Dacron nodded. Georgie whistled softly and remarked, "Guess we'd better prepare to meet our Maker."

Dacron looked puzzled. "My maker, Dr. Nubian Spittoon, is too far away for me to meet him in the next ten minutes. His laboratory on the planet Omicrowave Theta is—"

"It's a figure of speech, Dacron," Georgie interrupted. "It means we'd better get our affairs in order and say our prayers."

Dacron gazed at him curiously. "I have never heard you speak of religion before, Georgie."

"Oh, I do," Georgie revealed, "every time somebody tells us we've got less than ten minutes to live. It's just that I'm usually down in Engineering, so you don't hear it."

Zulu chuckled. "Sounds like the old saying is true: 'There are no atheists in black holes.' "

"If you'll excuse me from this philosophical discussion," Troit broke in, "I'm going to spend my last moments of life enjoying a hot fudge sundae." She headed for the Crewmover.

"I'm with you, girl," Guano declared as she followed Troit. "Let's crank up the sound system in Ten-Foreplay and go out with a bang." She glanced back at the others. "You guys want to join us?"

"No, thank you," Zulu replied. "I believe I'll go to my room and spend the next few minutes meditating, after which I will begin to scream hysterically."

"I'm staying at my post," said Georgie from the pilot's

station. He stood up and began to sing: "Rock of ages, cleft for me . . ."

Dacron said, "I will stay here on the Bridge also and explore a final possibility for increasing our odds of survival." As Guano, Troit and Zulu left the Bridge, Dacron rummaged around inside the storage compartment of his console, looking for his statue of St. Jude.

When the countdown indicated that there was less than a minute to go, the computer summoned all the Neuts back to the Bridge. When they'd all gathered there, the computer explained: "Starfreak special-effect regulations require a minimum of five crewmembers on the Bridge who, at the moment of collision, must simulate a jolt in roughly the same direction."

Guano suddenly went berserk. "I can't stand it!" she yelled. "We're about to die, and that computer is so . . . so . . . calm! Just like you," she cried, flailing at Dacron with her fists, "you . . . robot!"

Dacron held up his arms to ward off her punches. "If it would make you feel better," he said, "we can program the computer's voice to simulate panic."

Guano stopped swinging at him. "Yes," she said, panting. "Yes, it would make me feel better."

"Computer," said Dacron, "provide audio countdown to collision using '1117–17A Screaming Meemie' voice format."

"Thirty seconds to impact," responded the computer in an unusually shrill tone. "Oh no. Oh no. This is it. We're never gonna make it."

"That's better," said Guano, taking a seat in one of the command chairs. "At least somebody here sounds more worried than me. It helps me feel calm by comparison."

"Twenty seconds to impact," the computer wailed.

Guano relaxed in her chair. "Hey, computer, take it easy," she said. "It's not the end of the world."

"It is! It is! Fifteen seconds to impact," the computer shrieked.

"Boy, some people really get worked up over little things," Guano remarked jauntily.

"Hail Mary, full of grace . . . " the computer gasped. " . . . Five seconds to impact."

Guano yawned. "I think I'll take a nap. Wake me when we're through the rift, OK?"

"Three seconds to impact . . . " the computer screamed. "Oh no . . . oh nooooo . . . two . . . oh nooooooo . . . one . . . IMPACT!"

11

On with the Show

THE TIME-TRAVELING Pros and Cons arrived at Herschel's living room at the same instant. Herschel stared at them, pushing absentmindedly at the masking-taped bridge of the nose of his glasses.

Then the fabric of time ripped open, and they were gone again, plunging through the rift they'd created.

A half-second later, the Neuts arrived at the same spot. They paused only long enough for their predetermined action to alter the timeline: swooping up the Doritos from Herschel's snack table.

The computer readout indicated that this interference had indeed halted the black-hole effect, so the Neuts left at once, following the others into the future via the time rift.

Up ahead, a few of the Pros and Cons with their wits about them realized that neither group had accomplished its objective; Herschel still held Piker's videotape in his hand as they left.

But there was no time to ponder the implications of that. All they could do was hang on for their lives as they hurtled through the time rift. It felt like sitting inside a VCR that was being fast-forwarded. The Neuts followed, sucked along in their wake, drawing closer and closer until all three groups traveled as one.

The time-traveling Pros, Cons and Neuts arrived at Herschel's living room at the same instant.

Crash! The three vehicles landed hard, then began to vibrate violently.

"Get out!" yelled Smirk, pushing the Pros out of the Tardy. Ricardo evacuated his team from the funhouse. Likewise, inside the *Endocrine,* Dacron herded the Neuts toward the nosecone of the Bridge; they jumped out the exit and slid down the inflated emergency slide.

Everyone gathered nearby and turned back to stare at their travel crafts, which were vibrating faster and faster; the edges moved so fast that they blurred, then began wearing away. Soon their outlines disappeared. Then the middles wore away, until finally all three vehicles simply vanished.

The crewmembers became aware that they were not alone; a tremendous crowd of people surrounded them. Recovering from their shock, the crew looked around at where they'd landed.

It was a huge convention hall in a modern hotel. A banner off to the side read, "Welcome, Wrekkies."

The thought struck all of them, even Piker, at the same instant: they had been thrown ten years into the future, right into the middle of the wrekkie convention they'd seen on the Preview.

The effect was electrifying. The Pros began to cheer, jumping up and down and slapping each other on the back. And the Cons had a collective panic attack; some screamed and ran for cover, while others froze in terror. Only the Neuts remained neutral, reserving their judgment until they could experience the convention for themselves.

The crowd drew closer, curious about the newcomers who'd just arrived amidst the best special effects ever seen at a Getalife convention. One fan asked another, "Are these the 'surprise guest stars' we read about in the convention flyer?"

Dacron approached a pair of fans. "Excuse me," he asked, "but could you tell me today's Stardate?" He already suspected what it was, but he needed to know the precise moment so he could reset his internal clock.

"Yeah," said one. "It's Stardate 4149361212, and the time is 2:15 P.M."

"Thank you," Dacron responded.

The other fan touched the sleeve of Dacron's uniform. "Hey, great costume, dude," he raved. Then he leaned closer and added in a kindly tone, "But I think your artificial nose is a little too long."

Talking to the newcomers, the fans started to catch on that these were members of the actual *Endocrine* crew. The fans began clustering around their particular idols as the crew dispersed into the gathering.

2:17 P.M.

Piker paraded around the convention hall. He waved regally at the masses milling around him and entertained wonderful thoughts about being named Pope Piker I. Passing Smirk's autograph table, Piker gave Smirk a thumbs-up sign.

Smirk waved back, then returned to his autograph routine. With his felt-tip pen poised over a glossy 8 × 10, he smiled at the statuesque blonde standing in front of the table and said, "Hi, what's your name?"

"Charmaine," she purred, leaning forward until her curls brushed Smirk's forehead. She dropped her hotel room key into the box Smirk had set on the table; it clinked down among the several dozen keys that other classy dames had already left there.

The line of people waiting to reach Smirk's table snaked back through the expo area. His booth was like a magnet for every female at the wrekkie convention.

Even many women who were visiting the city for another, unrelated convention somehow heard that Smirk was here, and they'd joined the lineup to meet their heartthrob. Their severe dress-for-success outfits stood out in the crowd; it wasn't every day that the Sisters of Sorrowful Obstinacy left the convent.

His booth was like a magnet for every female at the wrekkie convention.

Near the end of Smirk's line, in another corner of the expo, Wart shouted at one of the vendors.

"How dare you sell these sacred Kringle relics!" he raged, pointing to a Kringle Electric Cattle Prod & Toddler Discipline Stick that retailed for $15.99.

"Hey, buddy, take it easy," the vendor whined. "Gads, some of you people really get *into* this stuff. These ain't actually the real thing, you know. I manufacture 'em in my garage."

"*That* is even *worse!*" Wart roared, lifting the edge of the table to overturn the vendor's wares.

Two burly security guards approached the booth. "We got a problem here?" one of them asked. They grabbed Wart's elbows to escort him out, but he flung them both aside like rags. Then, with a Kringle battle cry, Wart began smashing the booth with his fists.

A few moments later, more security personnel arrived. It took a half-dozen guards to restrain Wart. "Let's take him to the Green Room to cool off," one of them said as they carried Wart away. "Nobody's using it right now. The show doesn't start until 3 o'clock."

2:24 P.M.

Dr. McCaw panted, staring at the door of the janitor's closet in which he'd locked himself. As fans pushed from the outside, the door seemed about to give way.

With a final shove, they broke through. McCaw held them at bay with a scalpel. "Stay back," he warned, "or you're all in for some nonelective surgery!" They warily gave him a wide berth as he advanced through their midst.

When McCaw reached the edge of the crowd, he started running. The fans followed, but he eluded them in the narrow, winding service corridors of the hotel. A little farther on, he discovered the Green Room. With all those security guards standing around to keep an eye on Wart, the Green Room looked like a safe hideout, so McCaw sat down among them.

Meanwhile, Capt. Ricardo made his way unnoticed through the vendors' expo, disguised in a rubber Ferengi face mask which he'd bought for the manufacturer's close-out price of just $2.29.

Unfortunately, the mask didn't cover the back of his head, and a fan recognized his bald pate as he passed by. "Capt. Ricardo!" she trilled, pointing at him. Someone else squealed in delight. A small crowd gathered.

Ricardo, desperate to avoid their attention, bolted out of the expo hall. Searching for a secluded area, he too found his way to the Green Room.

2:33 P.M.

Despite Checkout's high hopes for popularity among the wrekkies, he soon realized that the line of people waiting at his autograph table was far shorter than any of the other Pros' autograph lines. He even overheard one fan tell another, "Well, it was either this or stay in the main auditorium watching that blooper tape, and I've already seen it six times."

Checkout burned with envy when he noticed that Zulu had to call on his old karate skills to fight off admirers.

Nearby, Troit felt another dizzy spell coming on. She hid behind a portable coat rack filled with discount Starfreak uniforms.

The convention experience had turned out to be a staggering assault on Troit's Betavoid telepathy. She couldn't help sensing that each fan harbored not only their own personality but also the alter-ego of at least one member of the *Endocrine* crew, and some fans identified with several crewmembers. It was standing-room-only among the personas, and Troit felt suffocated.

2:40 P.M.

Walking through the expo, co-engineer Snot spotted a tableful of Starfreak technical manuals that claimed to explain "everything there is to know about ship's propulsion." He freaked out. Paramedics were summoned. They carried him to the Green Room.

Georgie was able to walk through the crowd unrecognized, since he appeared to be just one of many fans wearing the plastic visor costume accessory that could be purchased throughout the expo. He got in line to tour a working model of the *Endocrine* that a local wrekkie chapter had constructed.

Georgie was amazed as he walked through the full-size replica; it was perfect to the last detail. Wandering around the reconstructed Bridge, he lifted the lid of Dacron's console and saw that the builders had even remembered to stash inside it a copy of *Soap Opera Digest*.

The tour ended in the Engine Room, and Georgie's astonishment increased; studying the dilithium Crystal Vanish chamber, he realized that this ship would actually work. It could really be used for space travel, as soon as they removed the velvet ropes preventing anyone from touching the control panel.

As he left the replica ship, Georgie noticed Beverage Flusher sitting at an autograph table. "How's it going, Doctor?" Georgie asked.

"Terrible," she snarled. "Most of the people stop here only to ask me where Counselor Troit is signing autographs."

A man in a business suit approached them and said, "Excuse me, but you're both from the *Endocrine,* aren't you?" They nodded. The man continued, "I'm a promoter from Getalife Conventions. Would you come with me, please?"

2:52 P.M.

In one corner of the Green Room, Yoohoo started warming up for her daily practice by singing scales. In the opposite corner, Guano got down on her knees in front of the security guard who'd brought her there. "Please!" she implored. "Earplugs . . . wads of cotton . . . even an old

Georgie was able to walk through the crowd unrecognized.

Kleenex—I'll take whatever you've got! Just let me plug my ears!"

The door opened, and the promoter who'd approached Georgie and Beverage led them and several others into the room. "Well, how do you like our convention so far?" the promoter asked, beaming.

"Sir," said Mr. Smock, "this is the most bizarre outbreak of human emotion I have ever seen."

"It's great, isn't it?" the promoter responded, slapping Smock on the back. "People can't believe their luck—seeing you all here in person! I just wish you would have told me you were coming so we could have advertised it. We probably could have charged a higher admission fee, too."

2:57 P.M.

"Captain, do you realize that all of our crewmembers have assembled in this room?" Dacron said.

"I know," Ricardo muttered. "Something odd is going on." He scanned the Green Room nervously.

The door opened, and someone called in to them: "Three minutes to curtain!"

On their way into the Green Room, some of the crew had glimpsed the huge crowd that filled the main auditorium to capacity. Now it dawned on them that they were going to be escorted onstage in front of this crowd.

Pandemonium broke out among the Cons. Ricardo wrung his worry beads so hard that the chain broke apart. Smock's startled expression lifted his Vulture eyebrow so high that it disappeared into his bangs. McCaw and Snot scrambled to hide behind Wart, who brushed them aside like sand fleas. Then all five of them made a panic-stricken dash for the door, but even Wart couldn't break through the dozen bouncers who blocked their way.

In her corner, Guano rhythmically thumped her head against the wall, wailing, "I'm not gonna share the stage with a singing Yoohoo! No! Nooooo!"

3 P.M.

The entire crew stood onstage behind the curtain, waiting for the big moment. The promoters told them that they'd be introduced to the crowd, after which they'd take part in a brief ceremony.

Some crewmembers tingled in anticipation of their moment in the spotlight. Others wondered whether they would survive the ordeal; only the thought of the bouncers lurking offstage kept them from making a run for it.

The chief promoter was onstage now, standing in front of the curtain. They heard him greet the audience: "Hey, everybody, what time is it?"

"It's Starfreak time!" they responded in unison.

"Have we got a show for you today!" the promoter continued. "This is a Getalife exclusive! For the first time ever, live and together onstage, ladies and gentlemen, welcome the crew of the USS *Endocrine!*"

The curtain rose. The audience roared, and all the crewmembers, even the Cons, gasped in amazement. It was an incredible feeling—this outpouring of affection from total strangers, people who'd previously known them only through the magic of videotape.

As the five-minute standing ovation finally started to die down, a woman called out from the balcony, "Can we come onstage and give you a hug?!"

Smirk stepped forward. "Sure!" he agreed. The crowd went wild, and only a phalanx of security guards at the front prevented fans from storming the stage.

After another long wait for the crowd to quiet, the promoter and another man came onstage and approached the two captains in the center of the group. The promoter announced, "And now I'd like to introduce Wade Beamer, president of 'Starfreaks and Proud of It,' the fan club here in Maplewood that's given us so much wonderful volunteer help at this convention. Wade will make a presentation to the crew." He handed the microphone to Wade.

Wade looked a little nervous. The microphone slipped out of his sweaty palm and clunked onto the floor. As he picked up the mike, he swayed a little, his knees knocking together. "O-n," he began, his voice cracking; he cleared his throat and tried again. "On behalf of 'Starfreaks and Proud of It,' and wrekkies everywhere," he quavered, "to thank you for making this historic appearance today, it is my honor to present you with the keys to our working model of the USS *Endocrine*." He saluted the crew, adding, "Live long and profit!" The audience cheered.

Ricardo and Smirk both reached toward Wade's outstretched hand and grabbed the keys. The captains did a little tug of war with the key ring for a moment; then, realizing they ought to look gracious while onstage, together they held the keys aloft. The convention hall vibrated with the crowd's ovation.

3:30 P.M.

Zulu, sitting in the pilot's seat of the *Endocrine* replica, turned the key. The engine purred to life. The other crew members at their Bridge stations sighed with relief.

"All systems go?" Smirk inquired. "Fuel?"

"Check," Dacron replied.

"Flaps down?"

"Check."

"Windshield cleaned?"

"Check."

Smirk nodded his go-ahead, and Ricardo ordered, "Engage."

Zulu touched the control panel, and the ship rose straight up and blasted through the ceiling of the convention hall.

A few crewmembers looked down wistfully at the convention they were leaving behind. As the ship rose higher, the conventiongoers looked like so many ants, including the chief promoter ant, who was shaking his head in dismay over the damage to the convention hall's roof.

After the ship cleared the building, Zulu switched to horizontal propulsion and kicked the engines up to Warped 23 in the Super Reverse mode. Bypassing numerous years, planets and commercials, the crew returned almost instantaneously to Ricardo's ship at the space/time coordinates where they'd started—way back to the moment when Smirk first thought of time travel as a strategy for getting his crew their own ship.

Smirk's team stayed on the wrekkies' working replica of the ship, while Ricardo's crew transferred back to their original craft. Everyone was happy with this arrangement, and they agreed that the timeline had turned out all right after all.

"But since we're back where we started, we've got to be careful to avoid getting sucked into the same sequence of events again," Ricardo warned. He and Smirk put their heads together to figure out how to keep from getting trapped in a never-ending time loop.

In the end, they realized that just one alteration was necessary. As they relived the day it all began, Ricardo simply refrained from asking Piker to set the clocks for Daylight Saving Time, thus preventing him from losing Westerly's tape in the abyss once again.

And to make doubly sure that the timeline wouldn't repeat itself, both captains made minor changes in their routines as they relived that fateful day.

This time, as Smirk started his memoirs, he wrote a different lead: *These are the times that fry men's souls.* And during lunch in Ten-Foreplay that same day, Ricardo ordered his standard meal of Earl Grape tea and buttered crumpets rather than venturing into sole food.

Within a few days, the corrected timeline asserted itself. Within a week, their bizarre time journey seemed like a fast-fading dream. And within a month, they'd all forgotten about the events that took place during the time warp—even Dacron, who erased the memory from his hard drive just to be one of the gang.

* * *

And so, happily restored to separate ships once again, the crews of Smirk and Ricardo blasted off into the sunset with a triumphant cry:

"Thanks be to God!"